PULLING AT THREADS

PULLING AT THREADS

Auld Reekie Scrievers

Edited by Gordon Lawrie

Dean Park Press

First published 2025 by Dean Park Press

An imprint of Comely Bank Publishing

ISBN: 978-1-912365-49-4

Cover art by Gerry Webber and Comely Bank Design

Text printed in Adobe Garamond Pro, Caflisch Script Pro and Calibri
by 4edge

A CIP catalogue record for this book is available from the British Library.

AULD REEKIE SCRIEVERS

Lesley Henderson

Norma Hurley

Andrew Licudi

Liz Logie MacIver

Chester Simpson

Sherri Underwood

Judith Wall

Gerry Webber

Olga Wojtas

Contents

Foreword by Colin Mortimer **1**

Andrew Licudi *Mimi* **3**

Sherri Underwood *Manipulation by Stealth* **15**

Liz Logie MacIver *Repairing the Damaged* **25**

Gerry Webber *Family Matters* **35**

Olga Wojtas *A Most Unusual Day* **45**

Judith Wall *Instability* **51**

Norma Hurley *Kalamata Olives* **59**

Lesley Henderson *Losing Grace* **67**

Chester Simpson *Who is Marion Shaw?* **79**

Sherri Underwood *Don't Listen to Them* **93**

Andrew Licudi *The Devil Sells Oranges* **101**

Gerry Webber *Angus Og* **113**

Chester Simpson *The Terrible Trio* **121**

Lesley Henderson *Alone* **133**

Norma Hurley *Taste in Friends* **143**

Liz Logie MacIver *Heroes of Our Time* **151**

Judith Wall *Old Spice Was Always With Me* **159**

Olga Wojtas *Hamlet and John* **175**

Acknowledgements **179**

The Auld Reekie Scrievers **181**

FOREWORD

Colin Mortimer

IT SEEMS A LONG TIME AGO NOW – I had enjoyed a very patchy and uncertain career as a performer/writer. But before that I had been a teacher in a primary school and a college of education. So, it seemed a natural progression to offer my services to University of Edinburgh to run evening classes in Creative Writing. They were called 'Write that Story'. And then for those who wanted more there was 'Write that Story 2'. But where did people go after 'Write that Story 2'? And so, back in 2011 or 2012 Stobie was born. I would run my own classes from home and call them Stobie. (Why Stobie? Well, the classes had to have a name, didn't they? And going round in my head was the song *King of the Road* in which the word stogie is mentioned. I liked it.)

So, instead of going to an anonymous classroom in a university building, we met in my large, warm living room and had tea and cake and discussed the stories people had written. Then, after the tea and cake we would have a think about a particular aspect of short stories, which people would practise by writing a short story for us to read and discuss at the following meeting. I just gave out some titles and off they went. And even though I quietly withdrew they are still going strong. And these stories are the result – absorbing, funny, moving, exciting. I know you will enjoy them as much as I did.

Mimi

Andrew Licudi

LE FIGARO ANNOUNCES
THE BEST DISH ON THE PLANET

Frédéric de Montigny, Food Correspondent

*'A reservation at Le Rouge-Gorge is hard to get. I've waited a long time to taste Madame Haxo's **'Betterave infuse à l'essence d'anémones et eau de mer.'** Haxo's dish is Lilliputian cuisine at its grandest. First, you're blindfolded. Then, with silver tweezers, the tiny dish is carefully placed on the tip of your tongue. At first, nothing, nothing at all, but slowly, as the essence of the ocean mingles with the earthiness of glazed beetroot, a chorus of beautiful mermaids bursts into song. What follows is an overwhelming desire for more.'*

I WAS SIXTEEN WHEN I FELL MADLY IN LOVE with Madame Haxo. She wasn't famous then, not even well known.

The summer we met had arrived early, making the nights warm as wool and the days bright and hopeful. I'd been gradually making my way to Paris after a lifetime at the Sisters of Mercy orphanage. At sixteen, we were evicted - no exceptions. Having no family or acquaintances, I reluctantly left with an address in the 9th Arrondissement, where a job servicing hotel rooms awaited. Hating making beds and cleaning toilets, I dilly-dallied, sleeping where I could, taking odd jobs, and delaying my arrival in Paris as much as possible.

On that fateful morning, I arrived at Monsieur Basset's market stall with his usual consignment of beetroots. 'What's a girl doing delivering beetroots?' growled Basset. Unfazed by his customary greeting, I dismounted my bicycle and unloaded his vegetables without a word. As I was leaving, Basset suddenly appeared startled, almost frightened, and, looking over my shoulder, spoke to someone behind me.

'*Bonjour*, Madame Haxo. How are you this morning?'

'I'd feel better if your produce was good. How am I supposed to run a restaurant with the rubbish you send me?' replied a woman clearly in no mood for morning pleasantries.

Turning around, Madame Haxo and I locked eyes, neither willing to look away. We must have lingered too long, disconcerting Monsieur Basset, who began swatting imaginary flies away from his vegetables. Despite her age (I later discovered she was in her mid-thirties), I immediately fancied her, as I was naturally drawn to faces with long noses and generous lips. Her accent was distinctly Parisian, though her tight jeans and straw hat covering her short blonde hair made her look like an English tourist on a summer jaunt.

'Who are you?'

Before I could answer, Monsieur Basset butted in, 'Looks can be so deceiving, Madame. She looks like a boy, but she's no boy. Her name is Mimi. She's sleeping rough at the Duval farm.'

Without breaking her gaze or flinching at Basset's revelation, Madame Haxo asked: 'How old are you?'

'I'm sixteen, Madame.'

'You look younger.'

I had always appeared young for my age and unusually pretty. When I was fifteen, I started to notice boys casually drawing near me, as if I wouldn't notice the fleeting brush of an elbow or a finger when we queued for food or exchanged schoolbooks. It was then that I butchered my waist-length hair with a pair of blunt scissors, trying to emulate the very gender I disliked.

'I've been looking for a pair of hands in my restaurant kitchen. Since you're young and lack experience, I won't pay you but you can have food and lodgings. It will be better than sleeping rough at Duval's. What you learn with us is entirely up to you.'

'There's an offer you can't refuse, Mimi,' said old Basset, attempting to ingratiate himself with Madame. Ignoring him, Madame Haxo continued to hold my gaze.

'If you want the position, come to the restaurant tomorrow at ten.'

With that, she walked away, but not before telling old Basset to send her the beetroots I had just brought. 'Remove the soil from those 'betteraves' before weighing them, Monsieur Basset. I don't want to pay for dirt!'

In a nutshell, that is how my unintended journey to become the world's most extraordinary chef began. Of course, I owe everything to Juliette (Madame Haxo to you), with whom I fell madly in love when she walked away from Monsieur Basset's stall. Then again, she owed her eventual fame as a restaurateur to me, so I suppose we ended up even.

If she felt anything for me when I arrived at the restaurant, she concealed it well. After she showed me to a tiny bedroom above the kitchen, I was soon assigned all the disagreeable jobs a restaurant kitchen offers.

Juliette was always distant with me, but I didn't mind; on the contrary, it spurred me to become indispensable to her. Through kitchen gossip, I discovered she lived alone in a spacious, sprawling house on the other side of the street.

I knew it would take time, but I was determined to be noticed by Juliette. I began to watch the old chef, Monsieur Kapelon, like a hawk. At night, when everyone left, I practised cutting spoiled carrots and onions into juliennes, batons, bâtonnets, mirepoix, and rondelles until each cut was perfect in shape and size. I immersed myself in old recipe books I found in Juliette's office. Soon, I was creating wine and port reductions from bottle dregs, small batches of stock from discarded chicken feet, and fumet de poisson from old fish bones. Whenever I could, I salvaged leftover food from plates and, alone at night, revived them with my velouté sauces. Pre

chewed steak with heavily reduced vinegar and sugar was a
revelation, as was tartare of turnips and fried chicken's blood. Once,
I boiled some discarded cigar butts, reducing the brown liquid until
only a foul nicotine syrup remained. The results were startling when
I added a drop of this noxious fluid to an indifferent boeuf
bourguignon, imparting notes of cedar, white pepper, oak, rare
grasses, and bitter chocolate to the dish. In my quest for knowledge,
there was nothing I wouldn't try, nothing I wouldn't taste,
sometimes making myself ill. But gradually, my little concoctions
began to taste astonishingly good.

It was two years before Juliette and I became lovers, and it all
came about when Monsieur Kapelon fell ill. Unusually, the
restaurant had been fully booked for dinner, and everyone panicked.
Even Juliette's nerves showed signs of fraying.

'Mimi, we are in a pickle. Monsieur Kapelon is ill and won't be
returning any time soon. He mentioned that you've often prepared
meals for the staff. Is this true?'

I'd never seen Juliette look so vulnerable, so kissable. I wanted to
take her in my arms and tell her she had nothing to worry about,
that given a chance, the food tonight would be exceptional, beyond
good. Of course, I didn't hug her or tell her any of these things.

'Yes, Madame Haxo, it's true.'

'He said you scorched turnips and served them with fried
chicken's blood. Monsieur Kapelon said it was *magnifique*. Is it true?'

'*Oui, Madame, c'est vrai.*'

'Is it also true that you made a velouté of oysters and tripe served
with a ceviche of mackerel skins? Did Monsieur Kapelon cry with
joy when he tasted it?'

'*Monsieur Kapelon est très gentil.*'

'You're young, and I wanted you to find your own feet. Unpaid
as you are, it seems you've used your time well. Now, I'm in the
unenviable position of needing your help. The mayor and his guests
will be here tonight. He's never thought this restaurant was good

enough. He will not forgive me if I embarrass him. Mimi, think carefully before you answer. Are you up to cooking dinner?'

'Yes, Madame Haxo. It's six hours before they arrive. I can do it.'

Juliette placed her hands on my shoulders, pulling me so near I felt the draught of her breath on my face. I was fainting with desire, and for a moment I thought she was going to kiss me before she brusquely pulled away and headed out of the kitchen.

'Do it, Mimi. For the love of God, do it!'

To impress you, dear reader, I should say how hard it was coming up with a menu, how tough it was to cook for so many people, and how the pressure almost killed me, but I would be lying. After all, I had secretly done it all a thousand times before, only now I had proper ingredients and the whole kitchen at my disposal. It was easy! I was like a child in a playground! More to the point, every time Juliette came to check on progress, she smiled nervously, looking for reassurance, and I smiled back and gave it to her!

When it was all over, Juliette called me into her office.

'Mimi, you should have seen the mayor's face when he saw the starter. Raw mackerel livers with popcorn, in a reduction of lime juice and soy sauce? How on earth did you come up with that? Of course, after he tasted it, it was all, 'Vive la France and long live French cooking!' she laughed.

I had never seen Juliette so happy. Once everyone had left, she opened a bottle of champagne and reclined in her chair, resting her bare feet on her desk. We were weary yet exhilarated, and the champagne had started to work its magic. Juliette said the evening had gone spectacularly well, and we were now booked for a fortnight.

'Mimi, I was thinking. My house is large. Why don't you move in with me? We could keep each other company. Could we?'

I couldn't believe my ears. I was sure Juliette would hear my heart thumping against my chest.

'Yes, Madame Haxo. We could,' was all I could manage.

Smiling, she pulled me towards her until our lips almost touched. Feeling her breath on my face, I inhaled deeply, desperate to take in the air she'd exhaled.

'Mimi, do you know why you can't call me Madame Haxo anymore? That you must call me Juliette?'

'Je ne sais pas, Madame.' My knees shook. She smelled of cut apples and warm bread from the champagne. I thought I was going to pass out.

'Because Madame Haxo doesn't do sex, but Juliette's a different story.'

At that moment, I ceased to be a wide-eyed rabbit admiring a beautiful big fox. Now, we stood on equal terms, for it was clear she'd wanted me all along just as much as I'd wanted her. What bliss! Laughing, we kissed, and I wondered what a reduction of her saliva in a sea bass ceviche would taste like.

Poor Monsieur Kapelon didn't make it back to the restaurant. He'd been a kind and considerate man. At his funeral, nobody thought it strange that Juliette and I held hands and cried. I felt guilt and shame that in front of poor Monsieur Kapelon's coffin, I was suddenly overwhelmed by a raw and urgent need for sex with Juliette. How could this be? Poor Kapelon would still be warm in his coffin! Perhaps my mind was befuddled by Juliette's tiny, black dress or the startling silver dragonfly pinned to her breast. When we got home, Juliette told me she'd felt the same, that it was known funerals made one yearn for life, and we should not waste Monsieur Kapelon's final offering. Kissing and clutching each other urgently, we stumbled up the stone stairs, leaving a trail of clothes and shoes behind us. When we finished, we lay in her large bed, exhausted and sweating, each with our thoughts on life and death.

'Juliette.'

'Yes, Mimi.'

'Your sweat is strange today. Do you think sorrow makes us taste different?'

'I don't know, Mimi. Perhaps it does. Is it unpleasant?'

'On the contrary. As a child, I thought that's how Adam and Eve's apple would taste like.'

'Would it be worth losing paradise for such a taste?'

'Yes, perhaps it would.' I looked over, but she was already snoring gently. Soon, I was asleep and dreamt Monsieur Kapelon was showing me how to make a white sauce from Juliette's sweat.

I'd never been happier. Since the mayor's visit, the restaurant was booked most evenings. I cooked what I liked. We were in love. Juliette used to laugh, saying I kept pushing the boundaries of what was edible and that our lovemaking was the same. She was right: I was obsessed with anything that could be felt or tasted. For her fortieth birthday, I was determined to cook something truly special. My dream of Monsieur Kapelon's fond blanc from her sweat had seriously shanghaied my consciousness.

Suffice it to say, Juliette's birthday dinner was a resounding success. Naturally, I didn't share the entire story with her. How could I? What would she have thought if I revealed that the paper-thin slivers of scallops with chicken fat and dill sauce would not have been extraordinary had I not added the heavily reduced sweat from my armpits (*sans deodorant*)? Or that the turbot with tamarind would have been mundane if I hadn't marinated the fish in jus – painstakingly collected over weeks from my unwashed toes after long days in the hot kitchen? At that moment, I realised I'd created a new form of fine dining of the most unusual kind. Juliette's reaction confirmed it.

'Mimi, I don't think you realise how special you are. Your cooking is now beyond remarkable. We need to get these dishes on the menu.'

I smiled and kissed her neck. 'Whatever you say, Juliette.'

'I think, Mimi, we should change the name of the restaurant. 'L'Auberge du Bon Canard' doesn't do us justice. I was thinking 'Le Rouge-Gorge' and we need to redecorate. It will be all red, with candles in huge candelabra and velour cushions everywhere. Can you see it?'

I was so in love with her that she could have suggested we open a restaurant on Mars, and I would have agreed.

Before long, Le Rouge-Gorge became famous. We were fully booked months in advance. Collecting sufficient sweat and bodily fluids from myself was no longer feasible. A madame from Paris would send me what I required. The range of flavours I could now create was astounding, as Madame had boys and girls from all corners of the globe, from Mali to Beijing, and Oslo to Singapore. Our dishes were regarded as extraordinary. My former bedroom above the kitchen now resembled an alchemist's laboratory, with glass alembics glowing softly over Bunsen burners, mortars with heavy pestles filled with powders and spices ready to be ground as needed, and countless test tubes, each meticulously labelled by country, ethnicity, sex, and the fluid they contained. Needless to say, I kept the room securely locked.

It was three years after Juliette's fortieth that my world collapsed.

'Mimi, we need to talk.'

I'd never seen Juliette looking so nervous. At first, I thought she was ill or had received terrible news.

'Mimi, I've been to my lawyers, and the house and restaurant are now in your name. I loved you, Mimi, and still do.'

I won't bore you with details. Juliette had fallen for a Swiss businessman, a regular. They left for Geneva that same day. I never saw Juliette again.

I cried for days before my sadness turned to anger. The restaurant staff avoided me. I despised our clientele – their sycophantic remarks, the pictures they snapped with their phones to show they'd been there, and the way they nonchalantly spent thousands of euros on dinner and wine when there were starving children in Africa. In my anger, I tore down the photographs of celebrities with Juliette and myself.

How could she have walked away so cruelly? I became fixated on showing Juliette that I no longer needed her, and that her success as a restaurateur was entirely down to me. I resolved to become ten times as famous as she'd been. I would elevate my cooking to an entirely new level. Now on a mission, I closed the restaurant and worked, demented, for months, only leaving the kitchen for a few hours of sleep. I experimented, tasted, discarded, and occasionally produced something extraordinary. Soon, I had more than enough recipes to reopen the restaurant. It was an instant success; newspapers and magazines soon made me a celebrity. Unexpectedly, Juliette sent me a cutting from the *New York Times*.

> *Mimi has become the most extraordinary and outrageous chef I know. I would say she is the most extraordinary chef that's ever lived. If another chef like her appears in my lifetime, I'll eat excrement.*

I laughed when I read it. The poor man already had, for in my anger and drive to push boundaries no ingredient was off limits. I replied to Juliette with a matter-of-fact letter listing everything I had used in my dishes. I wanted her to know she'd tasted more of me than she imagined.

When her reply came, it was simple and to the point.

'I Always Knew ☺'

Manipulation by Stealth

Sherri Underwood

I DID NOT MEAN TO KILL MY WIFE. At least I think I didn't mean to. But maybe I did. I mean we have been married for 34 years now, I mean, had been, by then and there are, I mean were, so, so many things.

But I'll start at the beginning. I am a retired ornithologist. My birds were crows. I spent a lifetime studying crows. You might have seen a few of my papers. They were often referred to in newspapers and magazines. *Left and Right Eye Dominance and the Use of Tools in the New Pacific Crows* and *Migratory and Mating Practices of the Piping Crow* were particularly well quoted. My wife took no interest in my work. She didn't like birds. She claimed she was a cat person although we never had a cat. Her slight aversion to birds, a mild ornithophobia, turned into a full out corvidophobia and I believe I was at least partially responsible.

What my wife didn't realise was how much she had in common with the crows I studied. Crows are cannily intelligent and they are known for holding grudges. Crows have long-term memories. Oh so many traits in common. Crows remember the tiniest transgression – whether accidental or on purpose. My wife had a whole list of these filed in her head. Forgetting to pick her up from the dentist over 20 years ago, the small wine stain I accidentally left on the sofa, forgetting to take the bin out on collection day in April of 2020. I could go on and on. Crows are also notorious for scavenging. My wife couldn't pass a skip or a rubbish bin without having a look and then a rummage if something caught her eye. Crows are beautiful. Their black feathers glimmer with hints of blue and green in the sun. My wife's hair used to look like that but latterly her hair looked ragged and grey. A bit like a crow's plumage in full moult. And her nose, well let's just say it became more beak-like with each passing year. These crow-like characteristics were what attracted me to her at first.

Eunice, that is – was – her name. She flitted about the house and much like a crow she would fluff up her hair and stare at me. Her eyes were round and beady and like a crow's had changed as she aged from a nice blue to a dirty dull brown.

Covid arrived just after I retired. In the beginning, Eunice didn't seem to mind lockdown. I was around and helped in the house a bit, did a bit of cooking. I did less and less as Eunice would squawk around me as I stirred the pots. She complained my washing up skills left something to be desired. So I started doing more outside in the garden. One day without telling Eunice I ordered a bird-feeding station. That's how it was advertised. I needed more to occupy myself. What a good idea, I thought, to study the birds in the neighbourhood, observe the power struggles between them and especially get to know my neighbourhood crows. I even thought that if Eunice would sit in the garden and watch these marvellous creatures she might get over her aversion. Was I ever wrong?

There was a knock at the door and it was our favourite DPD driver, John. I answered the door and greeted him. He asked me what I'd been buying as the package was large and cumbersome. I told him that it was a bird-feeding station and he remarked that it was amazing the government hadn't tried to lock down the birds as well. Then he chuckled and walked away. Eunice of course cawed from the kitchen asking what I'd bought this time. She was not that pleased when I told her. What I hadn't told her was that I'd taken delivery of Scott Pet Sunflower Heart (3 bags), Kaytee Fatballs (3 boxes) and Wagners Wild and Gourmet Nut and Fruit Blend (3 bags) 3 days earlier. At a weight of 20 pounds a bag I was lucky to catch John before he came up the drive. We tucked them away at the back of the garage so Eunice wouldn't notice.

After lunch I told Eunice I was going to put up the feeding station out the back. I thought next to the washing line as there was a nice patio area there where we could sit and have a cuppa or a glass of an evening and enjoy watching the birds. I'm not sure how pleased she was because she cocked her head and glared at me. She had taken to cocking her head and glaring quite a lot of late.

It was usually just me sitting out the back watching the birds. Eunice would bustle out, make a lot of noise to make sure the birds had flown before she would hang up the washing. The problem was the crows, canny beasts, only flew to the wall where they would watch her and wait for her to finish. She pretended not to notice but when she finished hanging the clothes she would look up at the wall, narrow her eyes and shudder a little.

Her fear got worse. We were allowed out for an hour of exercise during the lockdown. Eunice and I would walk to the beach. The beach was usually empty. We were walking along the East Sands, that's the beach near our house, late one afternoon. Stuck upright in the sand between the dune and the ebbing tide was a tall branch. Put up by some bored youth no doubt. It must have been close to two metres high. There was some netting attached. The netting was swaying gently in the breeze. A lone crow was perched on top. It was a beautiful scene and I said so to Eunice. Eunice, I said, look at that. So beautiful. But Eunice shuddered. Horrible things those crows she said. She looked as if she was going to be ill. The crow was watching us as we walked by. After we passed I turned to look back. The crow dipped his head at me, took flight and flew right in front of Eunice's face. I tell you I didn't think Eunice was capable of such a scream. And such a long scream at that. The crow was in the next county by the time Eunice stopped screaming. I just looked at her and asked her if she hadn't overreacted a bit. You and your crows was what she said. I bet you told that crow to fly into my face on purpose. If I am perfectly honest I did think as we passed the crow it would be interesting to see it fly by. But I honestly didn't intend it to fly in Eunice's face, at least I don't think I did. And that's another thing they have in common. Sometimes Eunice knows what I'm thinking.

The summer passed slowly. I got to know the birds that came to visit my feeding station. I loved watching them. The little tits and finches, two robins who continually fought for the territory. I saw a spotted woodpecker and of course a lot of sparrows. But my favourites were always crows. I gave them names. I know you would say they all look the same, but if you observe them carefully you can tell the males from the females (size) and like humans they all move slightly differently. My two favourites I named Lucky and Moll. An interesting fact you might not have known about crows is that they are monogamous. Lucky and Moll always arrived together, chased away the other birds and helped themselves mainly to the fat balls. They were the last to leave the station when Eunice came to hang the washing and they remained on the wall watching her until she was finished. I got the impression they didn't much care for Eunice. But maybe I was projecting. I still found the crows fascinating but Eunice's crow-like behaviours had begun to irritate me.

It was towards the end of July. The evenings were long and light. This particular evening was mild. I persuaded Eunice to take her coffee out and sit with me while I had my whisky. There were no birds at the station. See, I said to Eunice, they've gone to bed. Eunice gave a half smile and then her jaw dropped and her eyes widened. I looked to where she was looking. Lucky and Moll had appeared from the trees and were sitting on the wall. Don't worry Eunice, I said. They are Lucky and Moll. A very nice couple. Eunice looked at me as if I was mad and picked up her coffee and went straight back inside. I shook my head at my crows and said well you've done it now. They nodded and disappeared back into the trees. I finished my whisky and went back inside to find that Eunice had gone to bed.

No mention was made of Lucky and Moll the next morning. I started to say that the crows were just curious as we haven't been out much of an evening, but Eunice just cocked her head in that funny way she had and accused me of conspiring with them against her.

A few days later I was out back filling up the bird feeders when I heard Eunice scream. I ran back into the house to find Eunice standing at the window screaming and tapping furiously on the glass with a wooden spoon. What on earth, I thought as I looked from Eunice to the spoon to the window. There was a lone crow I didn't recognise sitting on the lilac bush outside the window. The bird was staring in and tapping the window with its beak. Eunice screamed, it's after me after me I tell you, all the while hitting the window with the spoon. I calmly took the spoon from her hand and led her away from the window. It's only a bird I said. It was probably just curious and wanted to know what you were doing. When you started screaming and hitting the window with the spoon the crow thought you were engaging with it. They are very sociable. I'll make you a cup of tea.

Being cooped up with Eunice was getting to me and not in a good way. Her beady eyes seemed to follow my every move. Every time I went outside she would accuse me of loving those birds more than her. And I probably did. I would go out and clean around the feeding station, didn't want mice or rats. Then I would clean the feeders and refill them. All the while Lucky and Moll and sometimes a few others would watch. I found myself talking to them. They would nod in response to my comments. More and more crows were visiting my feeding station. They had moved out most of the other smaller birds. Crows are like that. They don't take kindly to others.

Eunice had taken to putting her wireless in the laundry basket and turning Radio 4 on full blast before she would venture out to hang up or take down the laundry. Mack from behind the wall popped his head up one day when I was doing some weeding and asked me if Eunice might be going a bit deaf as the radio was very loud. I just explained to Mack that she had become a bit nervous of the birds. Mack just laughed and said I guess this lockdown is making us all feel like we are living in an Alfred Hitchcock movie.

It was one of those most glorious summers. The days were bright and the evenings were warm. I could occasionally get Eunice out to have a drink with me but not often. She said that those two crows especially gave her the creeps. I thought it was rather endearing that Lucky and Moll liked to come out of an evening and I told Eunice so. They are very sociable birds. Curious too, Eunice, I said, just like you.

One morning there was a small incident on the way to the car. Eunice and I were doing our weekly run to Aldi's. We were walking down our drive. It's quite a long drive and a bit steep. I heard some flapping overhead, and I looked up. Eunice looked up too. Four crows had come from the trees across the street and were flying in circles above our heads. Marvellous I said to Eunice look how the feathers gleam in the sun. Eunice was not having it at all she put her handbag over her head and hopped quickly down the drive and into the garage. She didn't speak in the car at all.

The sun moved languorously through the summer days. Eunice and I had established a gentle pattern. Breakfast in companionable silence. Then she would potter in the house and I would work in the garden. We ate lunch separately. Eunice told me when I retired that she had married me for love and money but not for lunch. Which I took to mean I was on my own when it came to lunch. Late afternoons we would take a walk, usually to the beach.

One night there was one of those short, sharp but amazingly violent summer storms. It woke both of us up. Eunice sat bolt upright in the bed and announced that this was some storm. I can't remember if I said anything but I do remember putting the pillow over my head, turning over and going back to sleep.

The afternoon after the storm we were taking our usual stroll on the beach. I was busy pointing out the devastation caused by the storm. The fence along the dunes had been washed away. I imagined a giant hand coming up from the sea and grabbing the fence and the dune it was protecting, gathering them up into a large fist and then retreating back into the sea. I was sharing this image with Eunice but she was not paying attention. She was pointing ahead and turned and asked me what that was. When I looked to see what she was pointing at I saw a large blackish form. I told Eunice it was probably a dolphin or shark that had washed up during the storm. As we got nearer we saw that it was indeed a shark, possibly quite young that must have been stranded by the storm. There were several crows feasting on the carrion. They were reluctant to leave their repast but finally we were too near for their comfort and they took flight. Right over our heads. I turned to Eunice to see how she was doing just as a large piece of shark flesh landed with a plop on top of her head. She put her hand to her head saying the damn thing's pooped on her but when she looked at her hand it was bloody. Then followed a scream to end all screams. Fortunately there was no one nearby. It was so blood-curdling I thought she might be being murdered by an unseen assailant. After that Eunice would not go down to the beach.

It was the twenty-third of August. I was inside sitting at the computer. I always pay the bills on the twenty-third of August. I heard some bustling in the kitchen. I looked up from the desk and caught a glimpse of Eunice with a black bin bag. I just thought to myself, Eunice is taking the rubbish out. I heard her open the door. I muttered under my breath, damn woman never closes the door. It was only a moment later that I heard Eunice scream. The scream stopped when I heard the thud. I went out to find Eunice flat on her back, eyes wide open. I now know what a death stare looks like in a human. Before I'd only observed it in birds. Not much difference except the size of the eyes really. But here she was, dead on the ground. I looked up and saw a murder of crows lined up on the wall. Lucky and Moll nodded at me as if to say *job done*. I went inside to find my phone.

Repairing the Damaged

Liz Logie MacIver

S ILVAN MATERIALISED SIX YEARS AGO. A mystical force of nature. When we moved into our Victorian family home in the heart of the south side, the house was in need of some work. Graham and I were in our 30s. We had stretched our finances to afford the classic building. He was a trainee lawyer. I was a poorly paid academic. We had grand plans for the place. Inevitably we would have to improve our beautiful new home gradually. The townhouse was on three floors with spacious rooms in need of decoration. Our children were growing up and were both teenagers. They wanted to make a mark on their own rooms immediately. Navy walls for Ellen and dark green for Josh. What was amazing about the house was the light from the park across the road which had a rich leafy assortment of horse chestnut, beech and oak trees. As the front of the property was west-facing, the sun blazed into the bay windows every afternoon bathing the two drawing rooms with a golden shimmering light. Like a painting, the winter sunsets of deep orange and gold streaked the sky above the rooftops of the square and the park.

There were a lot of quirky corners in our home which we adored, such as a cubbyhole known as the butler's pantry off the kitchen. The pantry had an old window looking into the kitchen, which we presumed was for the purpose of borrowed light. Inside the pantry was a large Welsh dresser with three drawers and three roomy cupboards. This piece of furniture had a date, 1890, neatly carved inside one of the cupboards. The dresser was cruelly painted in an educational green colour, as were all the cupboards. I had spied an identical dresser in the Georgian House in Charlotte Square and came to the realisation that this could again be a beautiful piece of furniture with some love and care.

Silvan's name was recommended by a friend.

'He knows everything about wood. He'll do a really good job for you.' She was very enthusiastic.

I rang his mobile and three or four days later he called back.

'Hi, what's the problem? I'm not Dip and Strip, you know. So don't ask me to take your doors away!'

His voice was surprisingly luxurious, languid, even soothing.

'It's a dresser actually. An old dresser in our butler's pantry.'

'Oh, one of those. Right. I'll come and have a look. Where do you live?'

I told him our address. Several hours later, he phoned again.

'Where the hell are you? I am on the bypass and bloody well can't find you.'

'Take the Colinton slip road.'

'Fair enough. See you soon.'

Silvan arrived in a battered old blue car. I saw him park over the road and sneaked a peek. He was tall with greying hair but his stride was of a young man. He had a beard and his hair was tied in a ponytail. He was wearing camouflage trousers and a tee-shirt in the same khaki green. He wore army boots.

He spoke as I opened the door.

'Nice house. Needs a bit of work though. Hi, I'm Silvan by the way.'

He had presence right enough. He was at least six feet four inches. Handsome in a mischievous way, with a twinkle in his brown eyes.

'Hi, I'm Ellie. Glad you could make it. Where did you come from? Out of town?'

'Wow, Ellie, you're a pretty yummy mummy. Your hair is like Titania's, all flowing and romantic.'

His compliment took me by surprise, but it was welcome. Graham had reached the stage where he wouldn't have noticed if I was wearing a bin bag. He had his head in books all the time.

'So, you came on the bypass. Which direction?'

'Down East Linton way. That's where my WS is.'

'WS?'

'Workshop. Let's have a look at what needs fixing then.'

As he strode through the hall he touched and stroked the wooden stair rail and the doors in the hall.

'Nice wood. Original, but stained badly.' He ran up the stairs to the first floor without a word. I waited in anticipation.

'Fabulous curved banister on this landing. Great touch.' He hopped down the stairs two at a time.

'What was this house?'

'It was a boarding house for the school.'

'That explains the green paint.'

When he saw the dresser, he smiled broadly.

'That's a beauty. Cup of tea?'

'Oh… of course. What do you take?'

'Three sugars. Any biscuits?'

'Jaffa cakes do?'

'My favourite. How did you know?'

He was charm itself. He took the drawers out from the dresser. Checked to see if it was fixed to the wall. He also looked over the whole pantry, including the window.

'OK, Ellie. Just because I like you and this seems like the sort of place I would like to work, I can make you an offer. Let's say… £100 to restore the dresser, the old window, and to put glass in the door here so people can see the dresser as they walk past.'

'Wow – are you sure? That's a good price. When can you start?'

'How about tomorrow? I keep my own hours so don't expect to see me early.'

From that moment, Silvan became part of our lives for almost six months.

It became obvious that Silvan worked at his own pace. He preferred to have someone to talk to while he worked. He always had several tea breaks. His excuse was that his throat became dry with the dust.

He would arrive anytime between eleven and two. Over the months, he told all of us his life story. He had been born into a wealthy farming family in East Lothian but had escaped and gone to London to study. There he had met the love of his life, Pomona, an Italian girl. They had a daughter together, but after two years the relationship ended. He was vague about the details of this break-up. He was still in touch with his daughter, Diana, who was now eighteen.

The restoration of the dresser was slow but it was clear that Silvan knew a lot about wood. He treated each section of the dresser with the care and attention of something he loved dearly. As the project took shape, he talked about bringing some mahogany handles with ivory insets for the drawers that he had in 'WS'.

Silvan talked about music and poetry a lot. He asked all of us about our musical tastes. Our family have an eclectic mix of heavy metal, drum and bass, jazz, rock and brass band music, but Silvan seemed to have a recommendation for all of us.

'Ellie, you must download Elkie Brooks. She is really 'you' – I know it.'

'Elkie Brooks? She's a bit past it, isn't she? What are you trying to imply?'

'No, it's more about the lyrics really. In fact, if you don't like her, Rabbie Burns is another recommendation for you on the same theme. There is a message in everything.' I was none the wiser.

Silvan recounted stories about his youth playing rugby or cricket, drinking pints of gin and other mad pranks he had got up to as a young man. Over the months he could be strange at times. Moody. Sometimes he definitely smelt of alcohol. Eventually it became clear that he might have a problem.

One sunny Thursday in May he didn't arrive until three. He texted to say he was coming. I volunteered to wait for him to arrive.

When he came to the door he looked as if he had slept rough in a hedge. As he passed me in the hall the smell of sweat and stale booze followed him. His eyes looked glazed, like he was under a spell.

'Ellie, tea needed right away please.'

He sat down. He looked weary and troubled. Spent.

'Are you OK, Silvan? You look like you've had a hard night!'

'Yep, you're right, I have. You know, Ellie, I'm not sure who I am these days. My dad invited my uncle round last night. We drank a lot of whisky. My uncle… he's in the army. He's so like me. Looks like me. Talks like me. Dad's brother. Mum and him were always so close. *Close*, you know, Ellie?'

'What are you saying, Silvan?'

'I am saying he's probably my dad. I know it. I feel it.'

'You probably just have a lot in common.'

'No, I know my mum had an affair, and I reckon it was with him.'

'I'm sorry, Silvan. That must be really difficult. Why don't you confront your mum?'

'She has MS now. It's too late. I don't want to upset anyone.'

'And your uncle? Can't you speak to him?'

'Look, I said it's too late. We don't open old wounds in our family. Stiff upper lip and all that. I wish I could escape. Start again.' He stood up and went out through the kitchen door into the garden. He lay down on the grass and stared up at the sky near the steps from the French doors. He lay in the shade of a lilac right next to the herb garden.

Our garden is a long, fairly narrow space. I have planted two apple trees, two plum trees and a white rowan and filled it with love. The top of the garden is normally bathed with sunlight. Graham laid a patio and together we built a summerhouse, painted it in pale blue. We call it Honeysuckle Cottage as it is laced with the plant along with deep pink tea roses.

Silvan seemed so sad, I didn't know what to say or do. I left him for a while.

He lay for a long time. I saw from the window that he had got up and was staring at the trees. He stood transfixed near our old lilac tree. The large tree was beginning to show its colour. It was an old tree with a gnarled trunk, twisted and grooved with the years like a beautiful carving. Some ivy had chosen it as a home and the trunk was woven with green leaves in patches. The tree had burst into bloom a couple of days before. There was a flourish of dark purple as a profusion of fragile lilac flowers had begun to appear. The smell of new blossom was divine. Silvan put his face into a large soft conical flower and seemed to take a deep breath. He stood there for several minutes.

I went out to see how he was.

He turned towards me and laughed. He was like a mischievous schoolboy. His face lit up. His eyes sparkled. I had never noticed how pointed his chin was under his unruly beard. His head was cocked to one side and he flicked his hair wildly. He really was an eccentric character – like no one I had ever met.

'What a glorious garden you have, Ellie. Being here always restores me. That old tree is a beauty. Rabbie would have loved it.' It was a relief to hear Silvan talking in riddles again.

'I'm so glad you're feeling better, Silvan.'

He did very little work on the dresser that day and took all his tools away.

We didn't see Silvan for several weeks after that. He came back finally and finished the dresser quite quickly over a weekend.

His invoice was handwritten in very intricate copperplate writing. It was like something from a bygone age.

We paid him in cash.

We didn't see or hear from him for about a year and then one Monday afternoon I received a text.

'Hi, can I come round for tea and jaffa cakes?'

The tiny blue car arrived. When he stepped out, he looked different. Still tall but his hair was cut into a style and the beard had gone. He wore jeans and an ironed white shirt.

We sat in the kitchen. He asked how the dresser had been and went to admire his handiwork. He stroked the wood as usual and looked really pleased with the finished result. He turned to me and smiled broadly. That mischief was there again.

'I've met someone, Ellie. She makes me so happy.'

'That's great Silvan. I'm pleased for you.'

'She loves the woodlands, too. We're soulmates.'

We talked for a while about his new life with Echidna, a young Greek student, and his plans to move in with her. They were going to rent a cottage near 'WS'. Silvan left that day and we have never heard from him since. Someone we knew told me a few years later that he and Echidna had had a baby boy.

'O were my love yon Lilac fair, wi' purple blossoms to the Spring.
And I, a bird to shelter there, when wearied on my little wing.'

–Robert Burns

Family Matters

Gerry Webber

S HE MARCHED INTO THE SHOP and ignored the customer at the till.

'I've left him, mum,' she announced.

I said nothing at first, not because I was shocked or upset, but because I couldn't remember who she'd been living with, although I knew it wasn't the father of her drooling brat, which I was glad to see she'd left with someone else.

'I should have listened to you, mum. You always said he was a shifty-looking bastard.'

I tried to remember which of the many shifty-looking bastards she might be talking about. Callum? Colin? Something like that, I thought. In any event, I knew there were two of them who'd been sniffing around her recently, and that they had similar names. I also knew that I disliked both of them more or less equally which didn't help me an awful lot.

'Oh dear,' I said at last, hoping that it might combine a hint of concern with a touch of motherly affection, not that I felt either especially. There was something about Shirley that grated on me. I'd never been able to love her.

'Yeah,' she said, as if we were having a proper conversation. 'He went too far this time, so I cut up his clothes and killed his hamsters.' Hamsters? For God's sake, I thought. Was she dating a schoolboy? What sort of a man keeps hamsters?

'Well, I'm sure he deserved it, love,' I said. Then, turning to the customer: 'That'll be £24.98. Thanks. Do you want a receipt?' She didn't. In fact, she seemed to want out of the shop and away from my daughter as quickly as possible, which is what I too would have wanted, had I been free to leave.

'You look a bit... peaky, Shirl. Have you been eating properly?' If the truth be told she looked dreadful, but she usually did - too much lip-filler, bottle-blonde hair, cracked nail polish (bubblegum pink) and one false eyelash, the other quite possibly lost in a tangle of damp and dirty bed sheets somewhere.

'I'm fine,' she said, obviously annoyed that I thought she looked anything short of perfect. 'I've just been to Burger King, anyway,' she added, as if I was about to suggest lunch. Lunch? With her? As if.

'Well, look,' I said. 'I'm busy right now. Why don't you pop round later for a cup of coffee and tell me all about it?' I was hoping she'd decline or, more likely, forget.

'Yeah, ok. I'll have to come round in any case coz I've left a few things at your place, as it goes.' I'd forgotten that she still had a key and was cursing myself for not having confiscated it the last time she'd visited.

'I'll see you later, then,' I said, not expecting that the things she'd left at my place included three suitcases full of clothes and a noisy pink runt which needed its nappy changing. She'd christened him Tyson, after a dog she used to own.

'Well, it was Calvin's flat, Mum, so I had no choice,' she whined. Calvin, yes. That was his name. The woman at the Council had told her that she'd made herself 'intentionally homeless,' so housing and benefits were out of the question for a while. 'I knew you wouldn't mind,' said Shirley, stubbing her cigarette out on the kitchen worktop. 'Just 'til I get myself sorted and that.'

Thoughtless. Selfish. Just like her father, I thought.

The following morning at breakfast, I saw her repeatedly swiping at the screen on her phone and assumed she was looking for a flat. It turned out she was on Tinder. It was typical of the girl, she was always looking for someone or something to make her complete - another lover, a pet, a child, whatever. A mother maybe, but tough, she had me.

'What do you think of *him*?' she asked, showing me a photo of a bloke that was old enough to be her father. I checked to make sure that it wasn't actually her father, but decided that this one had more teeth and a shorter nose.

'He's a shifty-looking bastard,' I said, and left for work.

———o———

'This is Cy,' Shirley announced, when I got back.

I was looking at a short, fat, middle-aged man with receding hair and a two-inch ponytail that flopped against the collar of his lumberjack shirt. What sort of a name was that? What was it even short for? Cyrus? Nobody was christened Cyrus, were they?

'And what do you do, Cy?' I asked, stressing his name to emphasise its stupidity.

'I'm a social media influencer,' he said.

I would have offered him an extra-strong mint if I'd had one on me, but turned to one side instead, as if I'd just seen something interesting on the telly. On further investigation it turned out that he was unemployed but occasionally posted videos on Instagram about the Marvel Comic film franchise.

Three months later, Cy moved in as well.

'We're a family now, Mum,' said Shirley, which was when I discovered that she was pregnant again.

'So why don't you and Tyson move in with grandad over there?' I asked, nodding towards the fat sod in the lumberjack shirt who was slumped on my sofa playing Grand Theft Auto.

'Kids aren't allowed where he lives,' she told me, as if that was the end of the matter. I could only assume that Cy had been living in a block of flats reserved for middle-aged men on the sex offenders register, which reminded me to check him out, just in case. I was surprised to discover that Cy was not, in fact, a paedophile, but oddly pleased when I found out that his real name was Simon.

'Simon, son, you'd look an awful lot better if you cut your hair short and stopped walking around the house in your underpants,' I told him one day.

Why I called him 'son', I don't know. We're the same age, as it turns out. Forty-two.

'By the way,' I said, 'feel free to use my Listerine. I got it from Poundland.' I didn't tell him that I'd bought it specially, or that it cost me one pound fifty.

When her new baby arrived, Shirley was very briefly delighted. 'It's a boy,' she told me, 'so we're calling it Fury,' which was entirely appropriate as it turned out. The latest devil-child was a constant source of pain and misery even when he wasn't being punched by his older brother, Tyson. It was in the genes, of course.

'It's just so stressful,' Simon confided in me after a while.

'I know,' I said. 'I remember what it was like with our Shirley. She was a total bloody nightmare.'

'Still is,' said Simon, laughing.

And that was how things started.

'Shirley, love, I've got something to tell you,' Simon said a few months later. 'I'm leaving.'

'Good riddance,' she shouted over the screeching noise that Tyson and Fury were making. 'I should have listened to my mother. She had you bang to rights as soon as she saw you!'

'Yeah, well. About your mum…,' he began, but I couldn't hear the rest of the conversation above the screaming and cursing that came from their bedroom.

Shirley can be a selfish bitch when she gets angry, and a mouth on her like an open sewer, too. Just like her father.

So, anyway, Simon and I took the master bedroom while Shirley and the two brats moved into the room at the back. Relations were a little strained at first, but once we all got used to the arrangement, it wasn't as bad as it might have been.

We're family, after all.

———— ⊙ ————

'I don't know why you're surprised,' I said to Simon six months later.

'Because you're a grandmother, for God's sake. Of course I'm surprised.'

'I'm forty-two, you pillock!'

It was typical of Simon, typical of men. They never really pay attention, do they? Either that, or they just don't care. Age is just a number, they say in the adverts. Well, not when it comes to biology it isn't. Nor when it comes to the law, actually.

'So what are you going to do about it?' he asked. I knew exactly what he meant.

'Well, I suppose I could buy some earplugs and an air freshener,' I said. I was sure I could make a better job of it the second time around. 'Why? What are you planning to do about it?'

As it turned out, he did pretty much as I expected. He grew his hair again and started playing FIFA 2020 in his underpants until four o'clock in the morning. At least, that's what he did until I came back from the hospital with the baby in my arms. 'Angela,' I announced. That's what I'm calling this one. 'Angela, my little angel. Here,' I said, passing him the child, 'she's yours too. She needs changing.' I knew he couldn't afford to move out. His options were limited. What could he do?

What he did do was to leave me for Shirley. I hadn't expected her to welcome him back, though I should have remembered that Tyson and Fury were playing havoc with her sex life, such as it was these days, and that she wasn't the kind of girl that would settle for fleecy pyjamas and a warm cocoa every night.

'It's like sandpaper, Cy,' I heard her say to the two-timing (three-timing?) bastard. The walls in my place are paper-thin. 'But I found some lubricant at Poundland the other day. Strawberry flavour. Your favourite,' Shirley said to him. She didn't tell him that it cost her two pounds fifty - desperate, disloyal bitch that she is.

Baby Angela won't treat me like that, I told myself. Not my little angel. But something had to give, so I decided to leave Shirley and the fat lump to it. She was a cuckoo stealing the nest. I needed out.

'I'm off to Mum's,' I told her.

'But you hate Granny,' she said, which was fair enough, 'and anyway, she hates you too. Doesn't she?'

———— ๐ ————

'Of course I don't hate you,' my mother said, when I arrived on the doorstep with baby Angela in my arms. 'Whatever gave you that idea?'

I thought about reminding her that she had quite literally thrown me out of the house when I fell pregnant with Shirley, and had told me - well, screamed at me repeatedly - that I'd ruined her life, destroyed her marriage. 'You're a filthy slut,' my mother spat. My father left as soon as he heard about the baby. He couldn't bear the disgrace, I suppose. Shifty bastard.

'No. I don't hate you,' she repeated. 'Besides, it was a long time ago now, wasn't it?' She spoke as if the passing of the years might somehow have healed the wounds.

She looked old, I thought. She was, I suppose, if you consider sixty to be old. Her hair was entirely grey and badly cut. Her skin was lined and blotchy. She was frail and jumpy, like a beaten dog. But she dressed like a teenager in skinny jeans and a pale blue tee-shirt. The cigarettes kept her thin.

'You should never have kicked me out, you know,' I said softly. 'I was only fifteen.'

'Well, things were different back then,' she replied. 'Let's not rake over the past, eh love? I've said I'm sorry, so let's move on. Alright?'

She hadn't, but I let it go.

'I'll get it right with Angela, Mum. Being a mother, I mean. I can. I will.'

'Angela,' she said. 'That's a lovely name,' and cradled her grand-daughter gently in her arms. 'You know who the father is this time, do you?'

I knew who the father was last time. That's what I should have said, but I didn't.

She knew too, of course.

A Most Unusual Day

Olga Wojtas

IT'S A TERRIBLE THING TO WAKE UP and find a horse's head on your pillow. It's even more terrible to find the head is yours, and that all of the rest of you has turned into a horse as well. I would describe it as Kafkaesque, except that it's much less terrible to turn into a bug, even a big bug, than to turn into a horse, even a small horse.

It would have been easier if it had been at the weekend, and I could have taken my time getting used to it. But at work, they have a thing about punctuality. True, I was saving time on washing and dressing, but it took me ages to work out how to get out of bed.

And going downstairs was nothing less than terrifying. I didn't see how I could manage it unscathed, although it fairly concentrates the mind to think that if you fall and break something, it won't be NHS paramedics at the door, but a vet with a shotgun.

Breakfast was a problem. I knew there were some carrots in the fridge, but I couldn't open it. Eventually, I managed to nudge a packet of porridge oats on to the floor and trampled it until it burst. The oats were nice, but I ended up eating a lot of cardboard as well.

Getting out of the house was even more of a problem. I'm usually delayed because I can't find my keys. This time, I could see them perfectly well, on the kitchen worktop, but I couldn't manage to pick them up, let alone get them in the lock. In the end, there was no help for it but to kick the front door down.

Then I didn't know whether I should be on the road or the pavement. I decided the best thing to do was to go through the park, which was an enormous detour. Even so, I would probably still have been on time by galloping if it hadn't been for the children.

A cute little primary school kid being walked to school by her mother said: 'Hello horsie!' and waved. What could I do except go over to her?

She was about to give me a pat when her mother grabbed her and started to drag her away, screeching: 'Don't touch that animal! It's dangerous!'

The little girl's face had been so open and happy when she saw me, and now it was all scrunched up, whether through fright or upset I couldn't tell.

'It's all right,' I said, trotting along beside them, to the mother as much as to the child. 'My name's Angela. I'm not dangerous. You can pat me if you want to.'

And the mother fainted clean away at the sound of my voice. Thankfully, the little girl didn't seem the least bit bothered, and started stroking my flank, but I felt I had to stay until I saw her mum begin to revive.

'Sorry, sweetie,' I said to the little girl, 'I'm going to have to go to work now.'

I had almost reached the other side of the park when a group of toddlers ambushed me, shrieking with delight. No interference from the grown-ups this time: their two nursery nurses were sitting on a bench engrossed in their smartphones. I was about to explain that I couldn't stay when one of the toddlers scrabbled in its backpack and produced a plastic box full of slices of apple. The oats really hadn't been much of a breakfast.

'Thank you,' I said. 'If you take them out, and put them on the flat of your hand, I'll be able to eat them more easily.'

All of them wanted to feed me after that. I got carrot sticks, raisins, grapes, strawberries, and a slightly under-ripe banana. One little boy was starting to unwrap a KitKat when I saw the time on a church clock and knew I had to run.

But when I got to the office, the doorman wouldn't let me in.

'It's me,' I said. 'Angela. I'm sorry I haven't got my swipe card, but you can see my difficulty.'

He wasn't even prepared to sign me in as a visitor, and panic at being late got the better of me. I jumped over the security turnstile and made it to the lift just before the doors closed, although I had to get someone to press five for me.

It was mid-morning when I got a call to go to HR. 'You've already been warned about poor time-keeping,' said the director. 'But not only were you late today, you haven't done a stroke of work since you came in.'

'I've been trying, really I have,' I said. 'Is there any chance I could get a keyboard with bigger keys?'

At lunchtime, I got cornered by the union rep. 'They gave you a warning?'

'It's okay,' I said. 'It was my fault.'

'Don't give me that, Angela,' he said. 'I'm not having this. Come on.'

And the next thing we were back in HR.

'This is completely inappropriate, giving her a warning,' said the union rep to the HR director. 'This is discrimination.'

'How is it discrimination?' asked the HR director.

'Haven't you got eyes? She's transitioned,' said the union rep.

'No, she hasn't,' said the HR director, giving me a sideways glance. 'She's still female. And she's not doing her job.'

'She's not doing her job because she's unable to do her job,' said the union rep. 'It's up to you as employers to make the necessary adjustments to her work station.'

The HR director shuffled papers on his desk, unnecessarily. 'You mean put some straw down?' he muttered.

'I'll ignore that,' said the union rep. 'It's up to you to resolve this or I'm going to the press.'

The HR director gave me what was probably intended to be a smile. 'I don't think data collection and analysis is quite suitable for you at the moment, Angela. Perhaps you could move into another area? Marketing, for example? We could use you as our emblem, like the Lloyds Bank black horse. Can you rear up on your hind legs?'

'I'm not sure,' I said. 'I'm still struggling to master stairs.'

'You could do television adverts,' he said. 'We could call it Straight from the Horse's Mouth. We'd have to dub you, of course, get an accent more in keeping with the image we're trying to project.'

'And what exactly are you suggesting about her accent?' said the union rep.

They're both talking over one another, using me as an excuse for a fight. I slip out of the room and they don't even notice. Carefully, with growing confidence, I make my way down five flights of stairs.

'Goodbye,' I say to the doorman as I soar over the security turnstile.

The automatic doors open and I begin to canter down the road.

Instability

Judith Wall

December 1907

I CAN SEE THE BUTLER THROUGH THE BANISTERS as he kneels beside Sarah, her poor head bleeding on the tiled floor. He's checking her pulse, making sure no spark of life is left in her. He takes his handkerchief out of his pocket and wipes his fingers, removing Sarah's life from his powerful hands. He'll come for me next. I know he will.

I'm used to moving silently. Madam's harsh words when she realises that one of her servants is breathing the same air as her, have trained me in the art of passing by unnoticed. I shrink back as he looks up and takes his first step on the long staircase. I slide away, keeping to the shadows.

Madam's bedroom: he'll never think of looking for me here. A kitchen maid like me would be dismissed immediately if she dared set foot inside. I hide behind the open door. Madam's shawl is hanging there. Its stale scent mixes with the sweat of my fear and churns my stomach. Empty though it is, I fear I will vomit. I look at her bed, all expensive silk and lacy pillows, but a chamber pot sticks out from underneath it. I look away. My heart is pounding and I strain my ears to hear his footsteps over the sound of it. One of his shoes hits against the other as he stops at the door, breathing heavily with the effort of moving his bulk upstairs. I hold my breath and wait.

He moves on. I breathe out and struggle to keep it quiet so that he doesn't hear me and turn back. I follow the sound of his progress along the passage as he opens doors and shuts them again. He's big and clumsy, so it's not hard to keep track of him. At last I hear his heavy feet on the uncarpeted servants' stairs and hear him going up to the floor above. I need a plan.

Sir and Madam won't be back in a hurry. The day following their departure brought heavy snow. They could be away for a long time. It's no good leaving the house as my progress would be slow, my footprints easy to follow, and where could I go? My only hope is to outwit him. At home they said I was too clever for my own good, but Ma said I'd have to go and work at the big house and Pa said, 'Good riddance.' Well at least nobody thumps me here. I haven't had a bruise since I left the village.

Madam has taken her maid and Sir has his valet. The housekeeper was given permission to visit her sister who's ill, and Madam has allowed those who have parents to visit them for Christmas. She was going away anyway. I'm not visiting mine, thank you. Only four of us are left here: poor orphan Sarah, now lying dead at the bottom of the stairs; Cook, now lying dead on the kitchen floor beside the contents of my stomach which were torn from me at the sight of the poor kind soul; which leaves Baxter, the butler, and me, Martha. I'll be next.

I hear Baxter now as the floorboards upstairs creak.

I have my plan: follow him so I know where he is and hide when necessary. The carpet is soft under my feet as I move along the passage, and I stop for a few seconds to enjoy the comfort of this part of the house. I stroke the silky wallpaper and look at the portrait of a posh lady. The doors are shut and I'm confident that he's upstairs, so I turn the handle of one door which opens on to a room with dark, carved furniture, and a pretty bed cover with gold thread shining from it. I daren't go in and lie on it, so on I go.

The lovely carpet goes on and on along the length of the house. At the end of the corridor, the servants' staircase waits behind a pretty blue door. It keeps Sir and Madam safe and cosy, away from the ugliness of the bare stairs and walls with flaking paint. I creep up, clinging to the banister to steady my tremble. I pause on the second top stair and strain my ears. His feet are clomping down the stone stairs at the far end of the corridor. What luxury this house has: staircases at each end of the building, even for the servants.

I ease myself round the corner and freeze. Oh lord, what's that?

He's stopped. His feet shuffle and, God protect me, he's coming back up, his feet loud and clear in the empty house.

Quick as I can I open the door to the linen cupboard and slip inside. Help, oh help me! What if he saw the door closing? I hear his shoes scuffing the bare floorboards and he's coming back this way. But no, he's stopped again. Of course I could outrun him any time. Should I chance it?

A handle squeaks. That's my room. Is he going to wait inside in case I go in there?

I make up my mind to go back down but then, oh no, I'm too late.

I hear him come out and the handle squeaks again as he shuts the door.

Please don't come this way, I pray. I press my damp hands together like we did at chapel.

He pauses. I pause. We stand there in the great empty house and the silence waits for one of us to move.

It's him. His feet scuff away. I close my eyes with relief and shiver all over. Exhaustion hits me. I move towards Sarah's room. Mine has the squeaking handle, so I can't go in there. He won't come back here, not to Sarah's room, not now.

I lie on Sarah's bed and breathe in the scent of her: carbolic soap, sweat and a hint of lavender. I'll stay here for a while. He hasn't searched the cellars yet. I know I might lose track of him but I'm so tired now. My body shudders as it relaxes. What a shame though. None of this needed to happen. I put my hand under the pillow and pull Sarah's nightdress out. I hold it close. If only she'd listened to me.

———o———

I couldn't understand what she saw in Baxter. Big and clumsy with such a miserable looking face, it was hard to guess what he was thinking. I warned her. I did. She didn't listen. That night when I went in with my 'Sleep tight', and she wasn't in bed, I knew then. I warned her again. Then when Sir and Madam went away she didn't come up at all. I went down to the basement to his room, listened outside and heard them. I could tell what they were doing.

I spoke to her yesterday and told her that it's me who loves her, not him, but she said that he'd asked her to marry him and she'd said that she would. There was no sleep for me last night. I tossed and turned, wondering how she could throw away everything that we've been to each other. We've been happy up here in these two rooms.

Side by side.

Two loving friends.

Two friendly lovers.

I got up early and went down to the kitchen to make a cup of tea. I'd just put the kettle on the stove when she came in.

'Oh good,' she said. 'Alfred wants a pot of tea.'

'Alfred is it?' I said, all sarcastic. 'Your beloved Alfred is he?'

'Yes, he is as a matter of fact.'

'And what about me?' I blurted out before I could stop myself.

She looked at me, eyebrows raised. She laughed with a great loud snort.

'Not love again, Martha. You didn't take it seriously, did you? It was just a bit of fun. Anyway, I've decided I prefer men. I've chosen Alfred and that's that.'

She said she'd go and look at the snow, and turned to walk away. How dare she laugh at me? How dare she turn away like that? A powerful rage took hold of me, filling my head with a throbbing pain, holding me in a vice of anger and hurt. Everything was red and humming. The faces of people who had hurt me appeared. The heavy poker that Cook uses to prod at the coals was leaning against the stove. I grabbed hold of it and went up the stairs after Sarah. The soles of her shoes made a tappety tap but I was careful to keep mine quiet so that she didn't hear me following. She opened the door to the entrance hall and went in, letting it fall behind her. I caught it and slipped through, my anger raging. I lifted the poker and brought it down on the back of her head with the power of fury. If I couldn't have her, then nobody else would. She fell at the first blow, nice and tidy at the foot of the grand staircase and I hit her again to make sure she was gone.

I was all of a tremble at what I'd done but not bad enough to hang about. I hurried down to the kitchen to wash the blood off the poker but there was Cook, standing by the sink, staring at that same blood. She lifted her eyes to my face and I saw her realise something. She tried to move past me but it was so easy to stick my foot out and trip her up. She was old, unsteady on her feet and she went over like a bale of hay. I brought the poker down on her head as the red rage roared on.

The anger cooled and the humming stopped. I saw what I'd done to Cook and my stomach emptied in a fit of revulsion on to the floor beside her. I fled to the first floor to watch through the banisters until he came. He'll hang. No one will believe that a slip of a girl like me could do this.

———— ◦ ————

Alfred Baxter lowers himself on to a kitchen chair. He wipes a tear from his cheek and averts his gaze from the distressing sight of Cook. He lays the journal that he took from Martha's room on the table and opens it at the last page to have been written on:

> *24ᵗʰ Dec. How she hurts me, spending this Christmas Eve in his bed instead of mine.*
> *25ᵗʰ Dec. The day is spoilt by her betrayal. I am so alone.*
> *26ᵗʰ Dec. I fear that if my jealousy gets the better of me I will kill her. She deserves to die.*

Alfred removes his shoes and leaves the kitchen. He takes a skeleton key from a hook in the passage and creeps up to the servants' floor. He inches his way along the corridor with surprising stealth. It has suited him, the better to keep track of their misdeeds, to let the servants believe that he can only move in a clumsy way. He has honed his hearing to a standard of excellence. He has visited rooms and examined belongings. He knows all there is to know. Alfred pauses outside Sarah's door and listens to the steady breathing coming from within. He inserts the key into the unused keyhole. Privacy isn't a luxury that Madam grants her servants. He locks Martha in. She's not as clever as she thinks she is.

The poker lies on the kitchen floor. Alfred has read in the paper that the police can use fingerprints to solve a crime. He puts his boots on and ventures out. The snow has stopped and the sun has come out. A walk to the police station will clear his head.

Kalamata Olives

Norma Hurley

S HE BUMPED INTO ME IN ALDI. It was a bit embarrassing really. For both of us I suppose. At one time neither of us would have been seen dead in the place. But needs must, and as I said to Irene my home help, frankly I'd rather spend my money in Aldi and save the difference for a night out or a holiday than give it to Waitrose. And really Aldi isn't bad – their wine can be excellent – and they actually do a rather good tapenade – Kalamata olives would you believe?

Anyway, I was reaching up to get a jar of green curry sauce from the shelf when I felt someone's arm beside me, reaching over for the red curry sauce. I turned and there she was, Audrey Banks. I couldn't avoid her.

'Audrey? Well, how are you? You're looking well.' She looked a fright actually, probably thought she could get away with it in Aldi. No make-up, hair scraped back, and – dear Lord – was that a fleece she was wearing? And leggings? I suppressed a shudder.

'Claire! What a surprise! I didn't think you'd be shopping in here?' She trilled that dreadful girly laugh of hers. Hadn't changed a bit. After thirty years, still as irritating.

'I just dashed in for a bottle of their cabernet sauvignon, it's delicious.'

She was looking in my basket with its jar of curry sauce and its packet of noodles and I could see she was thinking *where is it then*?

'Of course, it's impossible to come in here and not buy one or two other things isn't it? Such good value.'

She was looking me up and down then. Cheek. I always make an effort. Even to go to Aldi. I was wearing my shiny red mac which is a bit tight, I'll give you that, so it hadn't quite fastened over my sparkly blue jumper and the bright green trousers I'd picked up for a song in Shelter. I've always been one for a bit of colour. When I looked down at what she was looking at I could see the big stain on my jumper. What was that? Was that last night's stew? Why hadn't I noticed that before? Irene keeps telling me to wear my glasses but I'm a bit vain about that sort of thing. Then I noticed my feet. In my sandals. She'd probably think it odd that I was wearing sandals in October, but it's that bunion on my left foot. Nothing else is comfortable. Although I really should take off the nail polish. It's been on for weeks and it is a bit of a sorry sight. Even with my eyesight I can see it's chipped and flaking.

But she was running on.

'Funny thing, Claire, I was just thinking about you last week. I had a couple of the girls from our year round for a coffee – you remember Helen? And Paula, Paula Kovic? And we were nattering about old times as usual and we got on to talking about that amazing holiday in Kos that we all went on when we'd finished nursing school. Do you remember, that whole gang of us? When we were young and fancy-free?'

Audrey was counting them off on her fingers.

'There was Angie, Teresa, Katherine – no, Karen – Karen Goodison, Maggie, Eilidh, who else? You, of course. And there was someone else, who was it? Ah, I remember, Linda Paterson – she was mad as a hatter, she was. Do you remember her diving into the harbour fully dressed for a bet? After she'd drunk about half a bottle of ouzo! God we were wild that holiday. That was such a great year group we had. We had a fabulous time, didn't we? A holiday never to be forgotten.'

I stared at her. Nonplussed is not a word I usually use to describe myself but it certainly fitted the bill. I needed to leave.

'Well, so lovely to see you again. Must dash. I've got a chum coming round for tea.'

'Lovely to see you too, Claire. Actually, while I think of it, why don't you come along to our next coffee morning? It'll be at Helen's next time. I know everyone would be so pleased to see you. It's been so long, hasn't it? Listen, here's my card with my number. Can you give me your number or an email and I'll send you the details?'

I pocketed her card without looking at it and hurriedly gave her my phone number. I headed for till number four, straight in front of me.

'Till number four is closing. Till number three will be opening shortly.'

The queue for till number three stretched back as far as the tinned Polish sausages.

I couldn't wait. I put down my basket and pushed open the door to leave. My breath was coming in gasps. When I got outside I had to stand very still for a minute and breathe through my stomach to slow my heart rate. The nurse at the practice had shown me how. It'll help with the panic attacks, she'd said. Get the anxiety under control.

There was a woman sitting on the ground begging. She's always there. I usually ignore her. She asked me if I was all right. That was nice of her.

I didn't allow myself to think about it until I was in the flat, sitting down, with a cup of coffee. There wasn't anyone coming for tea of course. There never is. I don't get visitors. Unless you count the local volunteer from Age Concern. Which I don't.

Audrey wanted me to go to Helen's coffee morning. Where no doubt they'd reminisce about the good old days, and very possibly get on to that fabulous holiday in Kos – the holiday of a lifetime. And how everyone had made incredible memories. A holiday never to be forgotten indeed.

Except I'd not been there. Audrey had clearly forgotten that. I'd failed my final anatomy exam and had a resit so couldn't go. *That* year, that is. I did get to Kos the following year but Audrey couldn't have known about that. At least I hope not. Or does she know? Is this some kind of a trick on her part? To draw me out? No – surely not?

But now I have a dilemma. If I tell her that her memory is playing tricks on her she might get upset or deny it, or say I'm lying. That's happened to me before when I've had to tell people that what they think they remember is wrong. And it's very upsetting all round. Maybe she's got dementia. They say you shouldn't contradict people with dementia who misremember things. Just go along with them they say.

But if I don't tell her I wasn't there and I go to Helen's and they start talking about that bloody holiday yet again, someone's bound to remember I wasn't there and then it'll all come out anyway. And how embarrassing will that be for Audrey? And I suppose all things considered I really should spare her that.

The next morning I was calmer and more able to deal with the situation. I had a plan.

I dug her card out of my pocket and looked at it. Audrey Banks, Psychotherapist and Counsellor, and her number and email. Also a website, I noticed. She must have retrained. I've not really kept in touch with any of my year. I lived and worked in London most of my nursing career and only returned to Scotland when my parents had both died and I inherited their flat. Not long after the incident, that was. No husband. Lots of lovers which suited me fine. No commitments. I never wanted commitments. So no children either thank you very much. And definitely no regrets on that score. Being the doting godmother for a couple of friends' kids has been quite enough for me. But I must say I have not had a sad life. Nothing to complain about so far as that goes. Quite fortunate all in all.

I checked out Audrey's website. She seemed to be very professional. Lots of people singing her praises. And she certainly looked a lot better in her photo than she had in Aldi. Well, well. Good for her.

I thought I'd check her out on Facebook as well. She must be there surely. And she was. Of course I couldn't see much without befriending her and I didn't want to do that. But I clicked on her 'about' information and, limited though it was, I noticed she was now a widow. So Philip was dead. How sad. I'd been at their wedding and now he was gone.

I crossed to the sideboard and scrabbled about in a drawer until I found what I was looking for. A battered and torn envelope with a photo in it. I pulled it out for the thousandth time and looked at it with the same stupid smile on my face that it always provoked. Philip and me, arms around each other at a taverna in a little village on Kos, squinting in the sunshine, grinning inanely. The year after the girls' trip to Kos and nine months after Philip and Audrey had been married.

I know, I know it was wrong – we shouldn't have done it. But we did. It was a crazy, intense, short-lived affair. We'd started seeing each other secretly in Edinburgh, then Philip had been invited to a conference in Athens and I'd been due holiday, so that had been our opportunity to sneak in a long weekend together. And I deserved it. I'd been cheated out of the holiday of a lifetime the year before by being failed my anatomy exam. We split up not long after we came back from Kos. I think we both felt a bit guilty.

I put the photo back in the drawer and picked up my phone. Audrey answered almost immediately.

'Hi.'

'Hi Audrey. It's Claire. First can I say I didn't know Philip had died. I am very sorry. But also, just to let you know, I'm going to be away for a bit so I won't be able to come to Helen's do. Sorry about that. I'm going travelling for a while. Not sure when I'll be back.'

'Oh that's a shame, Claire. But thanks for your sympathy. Philip died six months ago. Quite suddenly. I'm only now getting round to clearing out his things – it's been so difficult. Can I ask you something, Claire, only I'm afraid my memory's not what it was? Were there any of the boys on that holiday with us? It's just that I've come across this photo of Philip and it looks like Greece but I certainly don't remember him being there. Do you? Maybe I'll ask the girls at Helen's coffee morning.'

Losing Grace

Lesley Henderson

S HE'S BEEN DOZING IN THE CHAIR for an hour or so, she looks so peaceful when she is asleep. She is still attractive, her short, steel-grey hair suits her elfin face. She insisted she didn't need any help to get dressed this morning. I rub my arm where she nipped me. She put her clothes on the wrong way but I had to stand back and let her. She has no bra on and her blouse is on top of her jumper. Her skirt is back to front, and she has a pair of my socks on and bare legs. I remember her wearing my socks with a skirt on when we were students and she would tuck her bare legs under her. She often used to wear a jumble of clothes back then, and it made her look independent and vulnerable at the same time – just as she looks now. I smile at the memory.

———o———

That man is in my house again. He's an old man who looks a little like someone I think I once knew with white hair and bright blue eyes which crinkle when he smiles, which he is doing just now. He has a bad scratch down his face which makes him look a little scary. I don't feel scared exactly though, I mean I'm only twenty or so, I can't quite remember, anyway I am so much younger than him. Maybe he's a friend of my Mum and Dad's.

———o———

I become aware that Grace has woken up. She is looking at me in that way she has now as if trying to place me. My heart takes a dive. I force myself to smile at her. She smiles back, a good sign. She accepts my offer of a cup of tea, another good sign.

———o———

He's asking me if I want a cup of tea. Maybe it's a hotel. I decide to humour him and smile back.

'Yes, please, a little... em... white stuff but no sugar.'

He nods and disappears which gives me time to look around. I realise it's not my home after all, my Dad's favourite chair isn't in the room nor their teak stereo and definitely no budgies. My Mum and Dad always had budgies called Reggie. It doesn't really look like a hotel though, it looks like someone's home. It's quite a nice home if you like that sort of simple, uncluttered look, it's got a name but I can't remember it. I'm more into a lived-in look with big comfy settees, lots of these comfy square things, newspapers and books scattered around.

He returns and gives me my tea. He's put a little vase with a ... anyway, some kind of flower on the tray which is very sweet but I don't like to tell him that I can't stand those flowers. There are two mugs on the tray. I prefer china teacups but I don't say. He sits down on the opposite chair and picks up the other mug. I feel that's a bit forward of him and I need to say something.

'Excuse me, but, em... are you a friend of my Mum and Dad's?'

He looks surprised and a little sad as if he is disappointed in me somehow.

―――― ⚬ ――――

Just as I sit down Grace asks me who I am. I feel tears prick my eyes. It's so hard when she doesn't recognise me, and of course her Mum and Dad died several years ago.

'Grace, I am your friend and I've brought you tea.'

Try and be general and non-specific is what they have told me.

―――― ⚬ ――――

Honestly! Does this man think I am stupid? Why is he not answering my question? Why is he being so.... what's the word?

'Yes, I can see that but what is your name and why are you here?'

Let's see how he can get out of that one!

―――― ⚬ ――――

I really don't want to antagonise her but I can only be truthful.

'My name is Bill and I live here.'

She looks shocked and seems to be trying to process what I have said.

———— ◦ ————

'You live here?'

He nods.

'So why am I here then? Do I live here too?'

'Yes.'

'Are we flatmates?'

He laughs out loud causing himself to choke as he agrees that we are flatmates.

Why would I share a flat with an old man? I don't like this at all, I want to go home. I stand up.

'I want to go home. I don't like it here. I don't know who you are. Where are my Mum and Dad?'

He stands up and moves towards me.

'Get away from me. You can't stop me!'

He turns away. 'I'll get your coat, Grace.'

———— ◦ ————

I go to get her coat and mine. Usually, it's easier if I play along with her, and by the time we get to the door she has changed her mind. Sometimes she insists on going out and it's best if I go with her if she will allow me. Mostly these days she refuses and then I have to follow her. Usually, she gets to the end of the street and then stops. She is often distressed when I catch up with her, and happy for me to take her arm and return home. On a few occasions she has resisted my help and tried to run away from me. Luckily the neighbours know us and some come out to help me get her back. She always used to recognise the house when we walked back, but that's gone now too.

'Here's your coat, Grace. Let me help you put it on.'

———— ◦ ————

The man is back and he is holding out some kind of quilt that he expects me to put on. Who is this man and why does he think I would wear a ridiculous-looking thing like that? What has he done with my donkey jacket and where are my DMs? I push past him and go into the hall cupboard where he took this thing from. There are lots of coats and shoes there but none of them are mine. My heart is thudding now and I feel a little frightened. I don't like this at all.

'Where's my donkey jacket and my Doc Martens? What have you done with them?'

I hear my voice getting louder and screechier. I see a toilet and I run into it, slamming and locking the door. I stand with my back against the door, shivering and trying to slow my breathing. Breathe in for four, out for four, or in for two and out for three, anyway I keep breathing. I realise that the man hasn't tried the toilet door which makes me feel a little safer. Given how old he is though I doubt he could break a door down. This thought makes me smile a little. I look around. This room seems familiar somehow. It's strange though that it doesn't have a mirror.

———— ◦ ————

Grace has run into the toilet and locked the door and I don't know whether to laugh or cry. This is a new one.

She was wearing Doc Martens boots and a donkey jacket when we first met, and her hair was cut really short just as it is now. I fell for her immediately. She seemed so different, so free and alive. She laughed at me wearing my Edinburgh University scarf, and I immediately felt foolish and naive. She noticed that she had upset me and apologised, and told me that in Freshers Week the previous year she was exactly the same. It turned out that she was a second year medic and was at the Student Union to help show freshers around. We were both from the north of Scotland, me Inverness and her the Black Isle. Despite her outward appearance we were both quite similar, a little shy and reserved.

She was going out with Graham when we met. He was English, from Cambridgeshire, and rolling in money. It seemed to me that Grace was fascinated by how different he was, he opened doors to another world. I know it sounds a bit creepy but I knew right from the beginning that I wanted to be with Grace for the rest of my life, so I hung around with her and Graham. I actually got on well with him and we are still friends with him and his wife. In fact they have been really helpful.

Grace seemed to sail through medical school, she was so bright and she helped me understand concepts I struggled with. I had to study hard but she seemed able to burn the candle at both ends. I remained quiet and shy but Grace gained in confidence and popularity. She made me do things I would never have attempted. She signed me up for the mountaineering club and ski club she had joined the previous year. I absolutely loved mountaineering and up till a few years ago was still climbing. Grace was more into skiing – she was fearless *schussing* down the steep slopes.

I actually lost touch with Grace for a while. She went off to a kibbutz when she graduated. It wasn't until a couple of years later that we met up again when we were on the same ward doing our foundation training at the Royal Infirmary. She was the same but different. She had travelled around a bit and had volunteered with the Red Cross in various places. She was more serious, I suppose, and determined to qualify so she could use her skills to help. In fact for a while she was a real pain in the neck do-gooder.

Anyway, this is not helping. Sometimes if I go out to the garden and give her space it helps her calm down, and occasionally she remembers me when I come in – although that's less and less likely these days. She can't turn the key on the front door, and I've put a bell on the back door so that if she tries to go out I will hear her.

I call to her through the door 'Grace, I'm going out to work in the garden. Is that OK?'

———— ○ ————

The man is saying that he is going into the garden. Thank goodness.

Now I need to work out what to do. I wait till I hear a door open and close and I carefully open the door. He's not there. I pick up the coat he brought. I wonder who it belongs to, I don't like it so I put it down. I do need shoes and I try on the shoes, They're ugly things but they fit. I go to the door. It's locked. There's no thingy in it to unlock the door. That horrible man has locked me in. He's kidnapped me. What is he going to do to me? I feel myself beginning to panic but I need to stay calm. I notice that on the table there's one of those things that makes calls. I pick it up and a photo of the old man with an old woman is on it. I press some buttons and see a green square with a telephone on it. I press that and see some names and numbers. At the top is someone called Shona. I'm sure I know someone with that name. I press the number and it rings.

'Hello'

'Please help me, I'm locked in a house, I've been kidnapped by an old man.'

'Oh, Grace.'

'How do you know my name?'

'I'm your friend, Grace. My name is Shona.'

'Oh right, Shona. Can you help me then?'

'Where's Bill?'

'He's in the garden and he's locked me in. Can you call the police for me?'

'I'll come round to you, Grace, and we can sort it out – OK?'

'How do you know where I am and how would you get the door open? It's locked.'

'I have a key.'

'You have a key?'

She has a key to this house. She knows the man's name. I don't like this. I think this Shona person is maybe his... oh, what's the word... partner? No, helper? Anyway, something like that.

'No, I'm fine thank you, I don't need you to come round. Bye.'

I press the thing to stop it and she's gone. I don't know what to do now though. I think I will phone the police. I know it's 999 but I'm not sure how to work this thing. I sniff and brush away my tears. Maybe I can get out a window or something. I go back into the sitting room. It has these full windows and I try the door. It opens onto a garden. I see the man at the back of the garden and I quickly go round the side and there is a wooden door thing. I try the round thing and it opens. I'm free. I run as fast as I can and stop after a little while and look around. I don't know where I am. I taste salt on my lips. I'm lost. I rest on a little wall and give myself a talking to. Just keep walking, Grace, and you will recognise something. I'm cold and shivering a bit as well so I start to walk and walk and walk…

———— o ————

Shona has just been on the phone. She's on her way round. Grace thinks I've kidnapped her again. I quickly go into the house and the toilet door's open, I look around but she's not here. The front door is still locked, I check everywhere but can't find her. I notice her shoes are gone but her coat is still there. I notice that the patio doors are open a little. Oh no! The door bell goes.

'Shona, she's not here, she's gone again, we need to go and look for her. If you go left, I'll go right and we can keep in touch by phone. She's got shoes on this time but no coat.'

'Bill, calm down, remember the last time she went walkabout we searched for her for hours and hours and never found her. When we contacted the police she was in the station. Someone had found her wandering around. The police said that if it happened again you were to contact them right away.'

'Yes, you're right. I just don't want to bother them. I don't want them to say I can't look after her.'

'Bill, your face is all scratched again, she's run away for the third time this week, she doesn't know who you are, she doesn't know me or any of her friends. I think you need to get more help, you can't do it on your own anymore. But that's not for now. Go and phone the police.'

'Yes, yes you're right.'

I ring them and after an age I finally speak to the right person who is kind and helpful.

'Shona, they were very nice and said that they would send out a patrol car, they still have her photo, and will contact me with any news. But I would feel happier if we went out looking for her too.'

'Yes, of course, I am happy to do that.'

We go in opposite directions at the gate and I walk up the street calling her name. I can hardly believe how difficult it has become. It started five years ago when Grace was 56. It was silly little things, like she kept forgetting words. At first it was more unusual things like the name for a rowan tree or a caterpillar and we laughed at that. But then she started forgetting the name for common things like the bin: she called that a plastic tub for rubbish. Or the word for socks, she said the things you put on your feet before your shoes. Then she lost her glasses and I found them in the fridge. All of these were quite endearing and initially she was good at covering it up. I became really good at covering things up too but it just steadily got worse. In our heart of hearts we knew. I tried to talk to her about it but she just got angry. Then she was just angry with me all the time and frustrated with herself. That was bad enough but then she started to lash out and hit me.

The diagnosis was not exactly a shock. A small part of me had hoped it would be one of the other more treatable conditions with similar symptoms, but that was the husband in me not the doctor. They did start her on medication to slow the disease down, and I suppose it did for a couple of years, but this last year she is so much worse. She obviously had to stop work and I stopped so I could care for her. I thought it couldn't get worse, but I am struggling now with her not remembering who I am and the ongoing aggression.

I still love her, I do, I have all our memories of our years together, but I've lost the person I knew and she is lost in the confines of her mind. We've really only ever needed each other. We both loved our work and never wanted children. Maybe it would be easier now to share the burden. Oh my god! I didn't mean that, she's not a burden, she's just... Shona is right. I need to get some help, I can't go on like this.

My phone is ringing.

'Hello, yes, it's Bill Smith, yes, that's right. Oh thank goodness you've found her, thank you. She's what, she's fallen? Oh, no. Right, yes, yes, I will meet you there.'

I should never have gone out into the garden and left her. This is my fault, what was I thinking? I've let her down. I need to contact Shona and then get to the hospital. I suddenly remember how dishevelled she is looking today. Oh god, I hope nobody is on A&E that would remember her. She would hate that.

I angrily rub my tears away. Poor Grace, my poor, poor Grace.

Who is Marion Shaw?

Chester Simpson

MAJOR STORMS WERE RARE in this part of the country, and the night of the great lightning storm of '83 was talked about for years. For two hours, forks lacerated the sky, each thread splitting into seams and veins too many to count. People in the village gawped up as flashes of light and ripping cracks of thunder came with thudding regularity. Many took shelter and refused to look at all, cowed by the brutal force of the pounding as the closest strikes seemed to shiver the air and shake the ground.

There was no rain at first, but when it did arrive it came in an unrelenting deluge that swamped the land for several hours. Water came at the small village of Hymanech from many directions. The surrounding hills funnelled surface water down towards the River Usk and its tributaries. Even before that arrived, the village's ancient drainage system was failing to cope, so that Bridge Street, running the length of the village and itself on a considerable slope, was transformed into a small river. Most importantly of all, the River Ythan at the bottom of the village burst its banks, as did the larger River Usk only half a mile away. Tidal surges can reach this far up the valley from the Severn estuary, and combined with recent wet weather, all the rivers were high in any case. Now, in only a few hours, the river water was up to the top of the single arch of the Ythan bridge, and the lower end of the village was under three feet of muddy water.

By daybreak the floodwaters had not receded, and the rich red soil washed down from the hillsides and surrounding fields had turned the landscape into a large terracotta lake punctuated by trees, telegraph poles and partially submerged cars and homes.

The early morning's sense of shock led to huge dithering and confusion among the townsfolk, but organisation gradually prevailed. By noon, a small flotilla of rowing boats and rubber dinghies, and men in anglers' waders were working their way round the homes and moving trapped residents to dry ground.

All the residents forced out along the Crystal Row on the night of the storm were present and accounted for, most of them with relatives in the village. One or two of them were still at the church hall. So, it was only on the second day that a boat passed along in front of the limewashed walls of this old weavers' terrace and found the body nestled against Mrs Williams' coal cellar. It was a woman, that much was indicated by her dress and one shoe. Even to a layman's eye it was obvious that, whoever this person was, she hadn't died the previous evening. The body was badly decomposed.

———— ◦ ————

It was four weeks since the storm and the police appeared no nearer to identifying who the dead woman was. Flocks of uniforms, CID detectives and forensic experts had created quite a stir, but the initial energy of the investigation had ebbed away. Lack of any information about her at all was considered by some the most suspicious element of the case. The pathologists in Cardiff had done their bit but hadn't got very far either. They couldn't entirely rule out foul play, for the state of the corpse made it impossible to be certain about cause of death. They believed the woman was between twenty-five and thirty-five years of age. That was it.

Into this informational abyss stepped the people of Hymanech who took matters into their own hands. Amid all the speculation – a murder, suicide, an accident? – what irritated more than anything else was the constant reference to the 'dead woman'. Needing some kind of identity, she became 'Marion Shaw'.

The origin of the name remained a mystery to most. Only a few knew that the source was the teenage daughter of Glennys Taylor who worked in the post office. New stories about this woman emerged almost every week, only for each one to be discredited and replaced by another. Fascinated, Madeleine Taylor had decided to create one of her own. Adapting the name from a novel she had been reading, she set about giving the woman a history.

Marion Shaw was from London originally. A brilliant student, she had opted for a career in the diplomatic service. From there she became involved in the murky politics of the Middle East which had ultimately led to her death on a bleak Welsh moorland. Madeleine's attention then turned to what kind of person this was, what she was like. Beautiful, of course. And certainly independent. She knew what she wanted from life, and no man had so far come close to providing it. There were always men in her life, but she kept them at arm's length. Right now, as she travelled into Wales on highly confidential business, she had two offers of marriage on the table, and was fairly certain that she would accept neither. She was an exceptional woman, of that Madeleine was in no doubt.

Inevitably, with both Bronwyn and Madeleine home from college for Easter break, it was a natural topic of conversation in the Taylor household over their evening meal.

'So, Maddy,' her father enquired. 'You've just been down at the cottages again, haven't you? What's the latest?'

'Well, there's a new theory that she was a gypsy woman. Apparently travelling people stayed near Ythan Cross a few months ago, so the Iversons and Mrs Jones have decided she came from there. Of course, this is their third explanation since last Friday.'

'It's funny but I've never thought of her like that,' said Mrs Taylor. 'I think she is – was – well brought up, you know, in a proper family. Very conventional upbringing, and she herself was quite prim. But she married beneath her station, some salesman type with gambling debts. And he persuaded her to take out an insurance policy, and then he did her in on their Welsh holiday.' Mrs Taylor recovered from her reverie. 'But I don't think we'll ever know who the poor woman was now.'

'Maybe we're not supposed to find out,' Bronwyn chimed in. Everyone looked at her. 'I mean, I'm reading this book at the moment where a young man, a complete stranger, turns up in this fishing village as if from nowhere. It's assumed he's been washed ashore from a wrecked ship. It's a mystery. But the real story is about the village, not about the young man at all.'

———— ◦ ————

Madeleine Taylor wasn't happy and, in her more irrational moments, directed the blame at a curious source. For her, Marion Shaw cast a sinister shadow. It started with her realisation that the persona of this fictitious woman was one she would happily accept for herself. Leaving out the tragic ending, of course. Then it occurred to her that she was clearer about the identity of an unknown dead woman than she was about Madeleine Taylor.

What was the big deal with identity anyway, she argued with herself? Other people went about their business. They appeared content with who they were, and didn't have fits over trying to be anything else. Why should Madeleine Taylor be any different? Who am I exactly? This simple question shook her, for the answer that she assumed would be readily forthcoming turned out not to be there at all. It was like opening a door only to face a brick wall.

She studied her face in her bedroom mirror. A stranger stared back. The wavy, dark brown hair; the healthy, freckled complexion; the grey eyes with flecks of brown (her mother's eyes, everyone was fond of saying); the fullness of the lips that normally pleased her, with a slight Cupid's bow that didn't – all these features now belonged to someone else. The stranger's eyes looked back and told her nothing.

'Got a spot?'

Bronwyn hovered at the doorway with her usual armful of books. Madeleine recognised the statement wrapped in a question well enough. Something like: I'm having to worry about tort law and all you have to worry about is your complexion.

'No. I was just wondering who it is you've been living with for the past nineteen years.'

Bronwyn had been about to continue along the landing, but stopped in her tracks and looked again into the room. 'That's a bit deep for you. You're not going all Sartre on us, are you?'

'The trouble with me is I'm two-dimensional,' Madeleine lamented. 'If I turned sideways, I think I'd disappear.'

'What are you talking about? There's nothing wrong with your figure.'

'Very funny. Ha bloody ha. I didn't mean literally. I mean the kind of person I am.'

'Why, what kind of person are you?'

'That's exactly my point,' Madeleine fumed. 'Even you don't know and you're my sister.'

'Maddy, are you all right?'

'I sat down last night and tried to write down who I am. I made a list. The things that make me, me. Everything I came up with was about other people.'

'Such as …'

'Such as I'm the daughter of Atholl and Glennys Taylor. Or I'm the younger sister who used to wear your hand-me-downs, and fancy your boyfriends, and tried to live up to your grades at school. Nobody ever describes you as my sister. I ran into old Mrs Jones in Tredelyn last week, and she said I was the best English student she ever had. That was nice until it became obvious that she thought I was you.'

'I still don't really see why you're making such a fuss about it. Now.'

And nor for much of the time could Madeleine herself. The feeling had been growing inside her for a while. Whatever it was had crystallised with the discovery of a dead woman. She was going to be another Marion Shaw if she wasn't careful. Not literally washed up beside a village coal cellar, but just as anonymous, without any identifying features, with nothing at all about her that would make people say, 'Remember Madeleine Taylor, the woman who ….' The woman who…what?

The matter was still on her mind when she was persuaded to walk a section of the new Offa's Dyke Path with her father. For the two of them there was nothing 'new' about it. Atholl Taylor had dragged his family up here many a time when she was a child, and told tales of

Mercian engineers a thousand years before, and of Silurian raiding parties long before them.

It was early May and the ancient hillside earthworks and embankments were covered in a rich carpet of flowers, buttercups in some sections, bluebells in others. By lunchtime the morning's haze was gone, and they sat in bright sunshine with their lunch packs on the gentlest of Offa's ridges. A scattering of sheep and lambs grazed indifferently to their front. At their backs, fortunately on the other side of a fence, a couple of young, interested bullocks puffed and snottered.

The Wye Valley was behind them now, and from their hillside resting place they looked west and down over a limitless patchwork of fields and hedgerows. To the north it was easy to make out the dark plateau of The Black Mountain and the beginnings of the Beacons. Even from this distance it looked like a different kind of world.

'Dad, what do you make of Marion Shaw?'

'Make of her? You mean, who she was?'

'I suppose so.'

Atholl Taylor looked at his daughter and was struck by how beautiful she was becoming. She always seemed at her best when she was outdoors and being active. On a hillside like this, wearing clothes that were functional with no pretensions to looking elegant. And yet in these circumstances, she always was pretty. When she had something on her mind, she tilted her head and caught the tip of her tongue between pursed lips, just the way her mother had done when Atholl first met Glennys. Her hair was the same shade of dark brown, and naturally curled at the edges. He knew that she hated that curl, but it was natural, and natural always seemed to suit Madeleine best.

'That's not really what you are asking me, is it?' he said at last.

'I suppose I'm thinking that I could easily end up like her,' Madeleine said, sounding gloomier than she really intended. It annoyed her to sound so melodramatic, but there it was. It was said.

Atholl looked at her. 'I think she was a woman who had a lot of bad luck. One thing after another. Maybe she lost her job or split from her husband. Maybe she was in serious debt, with no one to turn to for help. Or lost a child. I suppose I'm saying that she might have taken her own life.'

'That's so sad.'

'Yes, but it doesn't have anything to do with you. You won't find yourself in a situation like that, because you wouldn't let it happen.' He was tempted to add 'and we wouldn't let it happen either,' but he sensed that wasn't what she needed at this moment. This was about her.

Madeleine shook her head. 'You can't say that. Any of us could end up like her. It's all down to luck.'

'Maddy, there's always luck, good and bad. It happens to all of us almost every day, and you know, half the time we don't even notice it. It's just there and we cope with it and we overcome it.'

'Dad, there are problems and then there are problems. Maybe she had a serious illness, and there was no overcoming it.'

'My point is that you and your sister have something in you that makes you rise to a problem until you've found a way round it. Your mother and I have seen it time and again. You're right, we all need our health, but given that, you'll do all right.'

Atholl Taylor finished in a 'that's that sorted' tone, but he could see that Madeleine wasn't satisfied, and he began to feel a little flat himself. Her pensiveness and silences over the past week were the reason he had coaxed her into coming out with him up here today. They used to do this all the time when she and her sister were at primary school. Then they had outgrown it.

Atholl took a bite out of his cheese and pickle sandwich, and watched a hawk about a hundred yards down the slope. It was hovering, level with his gaze. Even the stillest of days was never completely still up here, and every few seconds it would sway and tilt one way or another to hold its position. It had its eye on something, maybe a rabbit, obscured from Atholl's view by the odd clumps of gorse bordering the lower edge of the field. The hawk had its own problems, mouths to feed, and it was solving them in the way it was equipped to do. That's what we all do, he thought, like the hawk. Then came the darker thought: just occasionally, and maybe only ever the once, you could find that you were the rabbit.

———— o ————

The door opened slowly. 'Wodger won?'

'Mr Rees?' Madeleine asked, hesitation in her voice.

'Aye, could be.'

'I'm Madeleine Taylor and this is Atlee. My sister Bronwyn said we could look round, and maybe help out with a few things.'

'Aye. Bronwyn. Nice gul that,' Matthew Rees said. "Eapsa things needs doin', now yue ask, but I'll get by I'm sure.'

Madeleine felt the door was about to close, 'You don't remember me, Mr Rees, but I was Yum-Yum at Tredelyn High the year we did *The Mikado*. You made all the stage props for us that year.'

Matthew Rees' face brightened at that. 'I remember. I enjoyed doin' that work. I went with my wife to see it and she cracked laughin' the whole night. It was a good show. Which one was Yum-Yum?'

He still didn't show any sign of inviting them in.

'Anything we can help with, Mr Rees?' Madeleine asked again and turned to Atlee. 'I can do some cleaning, and Atlee here has a strong back and plenty of muscles. Or so he says.' She had been giving a lot of thought to Atlee's muscles of late.

Mr Rees looked Atlee up and down with some suspicion. 'You'll be one of Hattie Jenkins' boys,' he said. 'You're like your dad.'

'I can't help that,' Atlee said.

'Don't worry, son,' Matthew said. 'Joseph was awright in my book. All these crwdd clecs in the village did for 'im, I'd say. A vicious lot when they get goin'. Carn abear that myself and I daresay nor could he. Couldn't blame him for leavin'. Yue were a crot of a boy when I saw yue last.'

'Yue might as well come in,' he said at last. Madeleine had the odd sense that it was Atlee who had made up his mind.

'Well, there's all these sandbags needs movin'.' He pointed down to the two makeshift piles by either side of the door. ''Ard enough movin' them afore the flood. Near impossible after. Maybe you could get them to my shed over there,' he said to Atlee. 'There's a wheelbarrow in there if you want.'

Madeleine could see that Matthew had swept out the kitchen and rolled up the carpet in the living room and swept in there too. The house still smelled damp and fetid. Perhaps he read Madeleine's thoughts for he said, 'It wasn't just river water in 'ere. It came up from the drains too. Think I'll have to get rid of my chair and the sofa.'

Atlee and Madeleine moved a lot of furniture and the carpet out into the air and sunlight, lifted the kitchen linoleum too, and for the next three hours cleaned away at everything that Mr Rees hadn't been able to get upstairs or off floor level before the waters poured in.

'Diws annwyl! It's six o'clock!' Mr Rees suddenly announced. 'Time for yue youngsters to be goin' afore your parents wonder wot's 'appened.'

———— ○ ————

Most of the Crystal Row residents spoke in the old way, like Matthew Rees. It was during her day with her father on the hills of King Offa that Atholl Taylor had pointed out the fragility of it all. 'Most of these people are in their seventies and older. When they go, a lot of the dialect will go with them,' he reminded her.

Home for her final term of the year, she had that then all summer to put her dissertation together. Right now, she felt crushed by it:

'English and the Immigrant Community' had seemed fashionable at the time she'd submitted her synopsis to the department. But she knew now it stirred nothing inside her at all. The Linguistics faculty seemed to be swarming with similar projects, she was already dreading her final year coming up in the autumn.

Then Atlee, the youngest and supposedly the wildest of the Compongolo brothers, had joined the clean-up effort and thrown in his lot with her and Bronwyn. 'You know it's funny how things have changed. Pretty cool really,' he mused one evening.

'What do you mean?'

'All these people in the Crystal Row. I didn't know who half of them were. There are one or two I don't think I'd ever set eyes on. A long row of geriatrics and widows with cardigans and strange hair.'

'What do you mean 'funny'?' Madeleine had her reasons for thinking much the same but with Atlee you were as well to be sure.

'It's all the stories they have to tell. Some of them as clear as day about things that happened sixty years ago, but what happened last week escapes them. All the things they experienced. I hated history at school, really hated it. But these people are history and there's nothing dull about it. When Granny May got going on the subject of the Strike and Churchill, she blew me away, she really did. War hero – pfft! And this project of yours at university: you could publish a dictionary.'

'I don't know....'

'You bet you could and there'd be a demand for it too. Do you realise almost everyone we've spoken to these past few weeks will be dead in ten or fifteen years? Think about that. And it's all right here on our doorstep.'

Madeleine laughed. 'Yes, Atlee.' She looked at him, and thought again about her dad. He'd said much the same thing. Maybe he'd had her figured out all along.

———— o ————

On the 6th October, exactly six months after the Great Storm, Marion Shaw was buried in Hymanech's Baptist cemetery. Still unidentified, and her body due to be removed from Cardiff's Western mortuary and cremated, it was the Reverend Cromarty, on behalf of his parishioners, who lodged a request to the authorities to take her and lay her properly to rest. A small service was conducted in the church annex.

To everyone's surprise, the annex was packed. Fifty-five people found their own reasons for paying their respects to this woman who no one knew. Initially there had been confusion over seating arrangements. People, by force of habit, left the front row unoccupied, though clearly there was no close family, nor friends or family of any kind. Eventually, the Reverend said that those standing along the walls should come down and sit in front.

Afterwards, the assembly followed the hearse to the graveside. It was a breezy but otherwise beautiful, early autumn day. Slightly later in the year than usual the beeches were turning yellow over the wall lining the southern boundary of the cemetery. Some leaves were flying about, but not many as yet. The mourners gathered and formed a horseshoe round the graveside. Mr and Mrs Taylor, along with Bronwyn and Madeleine, stood off to the right of the grave, no more than four yards away, but even here the blustery wind snatched away many of the minister's words as he delivered the final consecration.

The ceremony over, everyone made their way back through the grounds to the church entrance. A number made conversation in subdued voices. Others were absorbed in their own thoughts, and some examined the headstones lined along either side of the path as they walked. The names on each stone offered a small glimpse of the complex fabric that held this village together, the past to the present: with one more soul newly in their midst, a guard of honour by the dead for the living.

Don't Listen to Them

Sherri Underwood

Jᴇɴɴʏ Sᴍɪᴛʜ ᴀɴᴅ Bɪʟʟʏ Yᴏᴜɴɢ are sitting in the front seat of Billy's parents' green Ford sedan. They are parked at the end of the world on a glorious summer's night. The end of the world. Really should have been named the beginning of the world because from there the entire Salt Lake Valley stretches out to the south, north, and west. The flight path of the planes can be seen as they head north to the airport. Millions of stars look down on all the young lovers who park there.

Good kids. They are good kids. They know the teachings of the church but sometimes good kids don't listen to them.

Billy reaches over the console and kisses Jenny. She kisses him back. Somehow, looking back, Jenny can't really remember how they ended up in the back seat, or how their clothes ended in a jumble on the floor of the car. She remembers feeling elated and ashamed at the same time. Billy held her. 'Don't listen to them,' he whispered.

Three and a half months later 9:00 a.m.

My name is Mary. I am parked around the corner a block from Jenny's house. I am looking at her file while I wait. I remark to myself that she shares her surname with the first prophet of the church. I see her approaching from my rearview mirror. Slight, light brown hair, not yet sixteen years old, she matches the description in the file. She approaches the passenger door and I reach over and open it for her. She puts the backpack she is carrying in the well of the passenger seat.

'Hello Jenny, I'm Mary, I'll be driving you.' I put a smile on my face.

Jenny doesn't look at me. She looks down as she nods and gets into the car.

'The drive to Elko takes about three to three-and-a-half hours depending on traffic. You have been advised on the procedure?' My tone is neutral, non-judgemental.

Jenny only nods. As yet I haven't heard a single word from her.

'Do you want to listen to music?' I ask as I put on a gentle rock station. I don't wait for her to reply. We head towards the highway that heads west to Elko.

Had Jenny been smarter and quicker she could have taken care of this in Salt Lake. There are three abortion clinics that could have saved her and me this time and trip. However, the powers that be, male I hasten to add, have determined that abortions after twelve weeks are illegal in the state of Utah. For the young girls of Utah who are... I don't want to say stupid – perhaps uninformed or uneducated? – this means it is usually too late for them to take care of the pregnancy in their neighbourhood. Hence Elko. I have taken girls as far as California, by the way. Sometimes I put them on flights. I am allowed to escort them to the gate and I watch as these small, solitary figures disappear down the gangway. Because of course they can't tell their parents. The shame. The words of the prophet. This is what happens when you don't listen to them. And of course the young men. They are only kids too. I doubt they feel the pain or anxiety the young women feel. They take no responsibility and feel relief. Only relief.

It is mid-autumn and the weather is fine and dry. The trees, now painted with the autumn palette, are striking. We make good time along the highway. We pass around Tooele and Aragonite. Places nobody has heard of but locals, probably. We reach the Bonneville Salt Flats. I ask Jenny if she'd like to get out and stretch and look at the flats because they are pretty amazing. Jenny just nods so I take exit 4. I've been here with others before. I stop the car at the parking lot located at the end of Leppy Pass Road. We both get out of the car. Jenny looks up at the expanse of white. Her eyes widen.

'I guess you haven't seen these before?' I am always stunned how few parents take their kids to see something this amazing located at their back door.

'No.' Aha. She speaks.

'Let's walk out a little. We can have a taste.' I look at Jenny.

The salt crunches under our feet. I wonder if Jenny notices the unique smell of the flats. I bend down and touch the salt with my finger. I taste it.

'You should try it.' I smile at her.

Jenny bends down and touches her finger to the ground. She brings her finger to her lips. She smiles. More words.

'It tastes just like salt.'

We walk back to the car and drive on.

Elko, Nevada is a small town an hour by car past the Utah–Nevada border. A river runs through the middle of the town and what little vegetation there is borders the river. As we approach the town we see the trees in the distance, some still green, but everything else is yellow, gray, dirty and dusty. The clinic is on the outskirts of the town. I take the Idaho Street exit. Three blocks south then two west. The clinic is part of a strip mall. There is no sign on the door. It is wedged between a dry cleaners and a nail salon.

In front of the clinic there are half a dozen people: four men, two women. Some are holding signs. As we get out of the car a man points at Jenny and shouts 'MURDERER'. Two women yell 'We can help you. We can save your baby.'

I see tears run down Jenny's cheeks.

'Don't listen to them.' I put my arm around her and hustle her through the door. 'Here we are.' I turn and hope I smile brightly at Jenny. I pat her knee. 'It will be fine. You will be fine.'

Jenny just looks at me, her eyes wide. Her cheeks stained with tears. She is not yet sixteen. I wonder who the boy is, the father. These boys never appear, never seem to be part of the picture. No accountability for the boy, the father. Ever.

I let Jenny pass through the door in front of me. The door closes and the shouting stops. The room is mustard-yellow. Cheap plastic chairs line the walls. The reception desk is low. We approach the desk.

'Melody. How are you?' Melody is around fifty. She has been behind the desk for five years at least. A volunteer. I don't know her story but I suspect she has one. Everyone does. She is tall and graceful. Her light-blonde hair haloes her beautiful face. She greets us calmly.

'Mary,' she nods at me, 'and you are Jenny. We've been expecting you. Let me take you through.' Melody smiles at Jenny. She stands and puts her arm around Jenny. I notice how slight and small Jenny seems next to Melody. They walk around the desk together through the white painted door.

Melody returns and sits back down behind her desk. She smiles at me and I smile back. We do not talk.

It doesn't take long. I look up from my book when I hear the door open. Jenny is escorted by Dr Wright, one of a handful of doctors who volunteer at the clinic. I nod to her. She hands Jenny a small brown bottle and tells her quietly that there may be some slight bleeding for a day or two. If there is any pain two of the tablets from the bottle every six hours will do the trick.

I stand and greet Dr Wright. She nods and smiles. I open the door to the outside and take a look. Thankfully the protestors are gone. Sometimes they stay and we have to take the girls through the back. Not today. I let Jenny go first.

When we are seated in the car, Jenny bends over and puts the brown bottle in the side pocket of the backpack that she left in the car.

As we leave the parking lot I ask Jenny if she would like to stop for something to eat. I know she hasn't eaten since yesterday. That is if she followed procedure and I am sure she has. Some girls are starving and some girls aren't. I never can tell but I always ask. Jenny looks up at me and seems to waver so I do what I often do. 'Well, I'm starving and there is an In and Out just down the road. If you don't mind I'll get a burger there. They're the best. You can decide when we get there.'

At the window of the drive-through, Jenny decides yes so we order and pull into the parking lot. I watch her devour a double cheese.

I don't attempt much conversation with these girls. I let them decide. Some want to tell their story, some don't. Jenny is a don't so we drove mostly in silence. Occasionally I'll point out a bird of prey. Sometimes there is a jackrabbit, occasionally a deer. Mostly it's quiet, just the hum of the car and soft music. As we near Jenny's house I give my little talk. It's always the same. I try to make it sound unrehearsed.

'We are almost back. You know if you have any problems you can call the local clinic. Someone will answer the phone day or night. Feeling sad or depressed is not unusual. It's partly to do with hormones and it will pass. You should never feel bad about choices you make that are for your own interests. The words of the prophet don't apply to every case. Don't listen to them. The clinic dispenses free birth control. Go in later and talk to them about it. You will be fine.' Same spiel every girl. Mostly they listen. I rarely have a repeat.

6:30 pm

Jenny walks in the front door.

'Jenny? That you?' her mom shouts from the kitchen. 'How was the hike? Dinner's just on the table. Come join your brothers.'

Jenny drops her backpack by the front door and walks down the hall to the kitchen. Her brothers are already seated at the table.

'We were hoping you wouldn't be back so early.' Jenny's brothers speak in unison. Then they take turns.

'Yeah we were hoping you'd be lost and we would have to call a helicopter and then an ambulance would rescue you and Mom would have to go to the hospital to get you.'

'Yeah but we wouldn't want you to be hurt.'

'No we don't want you to break your leg or anything like that. It's just… then we could get Lucy next door to come and babysit.'

'We love Lucy. She lets us eat ice cream.'

'Don't listen to them.' Jenny's mother looks up and smiles. 'Sit down, have some supper.'

'It's OK, Mom. We stopped for a burger on the way home. I'm tired and dirty. I'm going to have a shower and read in bed for a while. I'll come say goodnight when these hooligans are ready for bed.'

Jenny walks back down the hall. Picks up her backpack and slowly climbs the stairs to her room.

The Devil Sells Oranges

Andrew Licudi

THE VILLAGE SQUARE IS LONG AND NARROW. On one side stands the public library, with large letters proclaiming 'Biblioteca Nacional'. Next to it is a small church, its doors already open, though it will be a good hour before its tiny bell summons a handful of worshippers. On the opposite side of the square, a waiter sets out tables and chairs outside a small café named 'El Moro'. A man and a woman have already taken one of the tables. The morning is cloudless and bitterly cold.

'Do you think the waiter has seen us?' asks the woman.

'I suppose he'll come when he's finished.'

'He could have acknowledged us.'

'We arc not at the Balmoral,' says the man irritably.

'I love the coffee in Spain, don't you?' she adds quickly.

'Yes, it's different,' says the man, still annoyed. He knows she's right; the waiter must have seen them. The square is deserted, after all.

'What are you having on your toast?' asks the woman.

'Olive oil and garlic. You?'

'Butter and jam.'

'You don't like garlic much,' says the man.

'I don't. It's strange how you love it yet hate garlic breath.'

'I don't like it in others. I'll be stinking today. I am sorry.'

'I don't mind.'

'I know you don't,' says the man.

'It's so cold. I've never seen ice by the roadside in southern Spain before,' says the woman.

'I still don't understand why you wanted to come now. January can be so miserable here.'

'They say that it's the cold that makes the oranges sweet.'

'Why is that?' asks the man.

'I don't know. That's what they say.'

'I can't imagine why that should be,' says the man.

'We should try the orange juice,' says the woman. 'Here comes the waiter,' she adds, smiling.

'Dos cafés con leche, dos tostadas, una con ajo y aceite y la otra con mantequilla y mermelada. Y dos zumos,' says the man.

'Enseguida,' replies the waiter, smiling.

'He seems nice after all,' says the woman after the waiter takes their order.

'He's okay,' says the man, feeling better.

The waiter soon returns with their order. Steam from their coffees rises idly in the cold air as the waiter fastidiously places plates and paper napkins on the table. The waiter smiles when he's finished. As he leaves, he looks around. The square remains obstinately deserted.

'I'm desperate for a coffee,' says the woman.

Not looking up, the man rubs a garlic clove over a large piece of toast. The warmth of the bread lifts the clove's powerful fragrance around them. He pours a thin stream of green oil over the toast.

'The garlic smells fresh. It is often stale,' the man says. 'What's the jam?'

'Apricot. It looks nice.' The woman's blue eyes glisten from the cold. She tastes the orange juice, and her eyes suddenly widen. She stiffens for a moment but then smiles. The man looks at her.

'What's the matter, Hoops? Is the juice all right?'

'Extraordinary,' the woman says, avoiding the man's gaze.

'You seem rather cheerful suddenly,' remarks the man.

'May I ask you something, Vin?' He chews his toast and nods, so she continues, 'Do you like me?'

The man stops chewing. 'You know I love you, Hoops.'

'I know you love me, but do you like me?'

'What makes you think I don't like you?'

'I'm getting old.'

'We are both growing older.'

'It's different for women. One sees many older men with attractive younger women. Rarely is it the other way around; love without 'like' can be so tiring – like swimming in treacle.'

'Would you prefer to be liked rather than loved?' asks the man.

'To 'like' is so joyful, powerful, life-enhancing. It's hard to feign.'

'You make love sound grim,' remarks the man, taking another bite of his toast.

'Love is so demanding. It can hold you up on so many levels. It's a poor substitute for liking,' she replies, gazing down at her coffee.

'Well, this fool loves you, Hoops,' says the man, placing his last piece of toast in his mouth. 'In any case, you haven't aged in twenty years since I first saw you through the railings of that God-forsaken cemetery. People are beginning to wonder how you do it.'

They finish their meal, each deep in their thoughts. Neither speaks until the waiter appears like a ghost by their side.

'*Necesitais algo mas?*' asks the waiter, wanting to know if they want anything else.

'*No gracias. La cuenta por favor.*'

'*Son, 8 euros,*' replies the waiter as he clears the table.

'Vin, ask him where they buy their oranges? I've never tasted orange juice like this.'

'Hoops, endless orange groves surround us. They are sold everywhere. The chap will think I am a fool.'

'I'll ask if you don't.'

'You don't speak Spanish.'

'Enough to make myself understood.'

'Okay,' says the man. '*A mi mujer le ha gustado mucho el zumo. Dónde compran ustedes las naranjas?*' he asks. The woman watches the waiter pointing towards the town's entrance. She catches the words *Pedro* and *kilometro*.

'He says they get their oranges from Pedro. We must turn left outside the village, then take the first left, past the blue warehouse. He says Pedro will be there now. He is always there.'

'Why is everyone in Spain called Pedro?' asks the woman when the waiter leaves.

'Spaniards don't care for fancy names. Thank goodness for that. Imagine buying oranges from someone named Torquil.' The woman smiles and blows warm air into her chilly hands. Outside the village, the narrow, tree-lined road stretches like an arrow into the distance. There are no other vehicles. 'It's strange.'

'What's strange, Vin?'

'The waiter.'

'What about the waiter?'

'He said we shouldn't linger around here too long. Not after dark.'

'Why?'

'He didn't say.'

'Country folk can be so superstitious, especially in winter when it's cold and the days draw in early. There's the warehouse now; I can see the dirt track on the left,' says the woman cheerfully. 'Look, there's a neat pile of oranges by the side of the track – better than a signpost,' she adds. Turning into the dirt track, they soon arrive at a whitewashed hut. Its clay-tiled roof appears ancient and dilapidated. Blue smoke rises lazily from the chimney into the windless morning. A green metal door stands wide open. Inside, an old man sits by a roaring fire. He rises and smiles when he sees the young couple in their car.

'*Hola, buenos dias, sois ingleses?*'

'*Si, ingleses. Buenos dias.*'

'Why did you say we are English?' asks the woman.

'He asked if we were English and it's easier to say yes. To them, we are all the same.'

'Venimos a comprar naranjas,' says the man.

'I've told him we want to buy oranges. He says we've come to the right place.'

Inside, the scent of smoke is sweet, and the fire is warm and welcoming. Boxes overflow with large, bright oranges. Cast-iron scales rest on a rickety table. Dusty cowbells and an ancient, rusty plough hang on one wall. Another metal door at the back leads into an orange grove stretching into the horizon.

'It's a lovely fire,' says the woman, extending her hands towards the bright flames.

'Acérquense señora. Hace mucho frío esta mañana.'

'He says to go nearer the fire. It's very cold this morning.'

The woman smiles at the old man. Going too near the fire, she doesn't notice the flames licking her hands. The man pulls her back. 'Hoops, be careful! You'll burn yourself!'

'La señora es muy guapa. Tienes unos ojos muy azules,' says the old man, smiling.

'He says you are beautiful. You have very blue eyes.'

'Gracias,' says the woman, smiling at the old man.

'I think he likes you, Hoops. Your eyes do look rather blue today.'

'Afuera, la fruta es muy buena. Escoger la que queráis,' says the old man, holding out an old, plastic bag.

'He says there's good fruit outside. We are to pick our own. It's rather silly, though; so many are already picked here. I'll tell him we'll have some of these,' says the man.

'No, Vin, let's do as he says,' replies the woman, squeezing the man's arm.

'Hoops, you are hurting me. I didn't know you were so strong!'

'Sorry, Vin.'

The old man quickly ushers them towards the open door leading into the orange grove. He noisily shuts the metal door behind them, a bolt clanging into place. Orange trees stretch in parallel lines as far as the eye can see. There's grass between the dew-covered trees, and because the sun is quickly melting the ice on the ground, it's damp underfoot.

'My feet are getting wet,' says the woman as they walk among the trees.

'Mine too,' replies the man, 'I don't suppose there's much point in going further. All the trees look the same.'

'It's wonderful. Look at the fruit, all within reach. The leaves are so green and shiny. Look, Vin, this tree has only one orange, but it's the largest orange I've ever seen.'

'It's magnificent!' says the man.

'Why don't we eat it here? I am sure it's lovely, like out of the fridge,' says the woman.

'Hoops, we can't eat it without paying for it.'

'Why not?'

'Because we'd be cheating the old man.'

'Vin, look around you. There must be a million oranges. He won't miss one.'

'Okay, let's eat it, but I'll tell the old man and pay for it.'

'Vin, if I know you'll tell him, it won't taste the same.'

'What's got into you, Hoops? It's not like you. You look different.'

'I feel different,' says the woman, looking at the tree. The woman tugs at the orange sharply, but the branch refuses to let go of the fruit. When the branch yields, it snaps back, drenching the woman with freezing water. The woman laughs.

'Hoops, you are drenched!'

'It feels great!' says the woman, pushing her thumb into the orange. The skin is thick but yields easily. Soon, she is digging her sharp nails into its flesh.

'Here, Vin. Take this,' she says, holding dripping pieces of fruit. The man takes it hesitantly. She quickly bites into the flesh, forcing it into her mouth with her hands. The cold juice runs down her cheeks and neck. It runs between her fingers and down her sleeves. The man watches open-mouthed.

'Isn't this wonderful?' says the woman grinning. 'Eat Vin. You'll love it.' He eats reluctantly at first, but soon he too starts wolfing down the flesh. They stare at each other. They laugh. Juice runs down their lips. When they finish, they are out of breath.

'What was that all about?' asks the man.

'Who cares? It was wonderful. Forbidden fruit can taste so wicked.'

'You are right, Hoops. It was incredible.' The woman pulls the man roughly towards her by his collar. She kisses him deeply. Their tongues feel sweet and slippery.

'Give me the car keys. I'm driving from now on,' she says, laughing. The man, eyes glinting, pulls out several keys and hands them to her. When they reach the iron door, she bangs forcefully with her fist. The door quickly opens. The old man smiles when he sees their empty bag.

'Vin, I want to tell him it's a wonderful orange grove, but I know you'll make fun of my Spanish. Please wait outside.' The man laughs.

'All right, I'll wait for you by the car.' The woman and the old man watch him as he walks towards the car. It is not until he's out of earshot that they begin to speak.

'You found me,' says the old man in a guttural, long-forgotten tongue.

'How could I not? You left me so many signposts. The orange juice was a surprise, and I didn't expect you to be called Pedro!'

'One has to improvise.'

'You are always convincing,' replies the woman.

'*You found the tree, I see,*' says the old man.

'*Yes.*'

'*Another day or two, and the fruit would have dropped. You'd have been too late,*' says the old man.

'*I was held up.*'

'*You might have died.*'

'*But I didn't,*' replies the woman.

'*You've always enjoyed taking risks. Your eyes tell me you haven't eaten for some time; they ought to be black as night,*' remarks the old man.

'*I haven't eaten for twenty years. Being loved weakened me and took my hunger away,*' says the woman.

'*He'll never love again, not now he's eaten from the tree,*' says the old man, looking towards the car. Smiling, the woman nods and turns to walk away.

'*Lucifera!*'

She turns to look at the old man. '*Yes, Papa?*'

'*Sooner or later, you'll need the tree again,*' says the old man. '*In a hundred years, give or take a day. Don't cut it so finely next time.*'

'*I suppose you won't be here long?*' says the woman.

'*I'll have to move soon. You know what it's like.*'

'*It will be fun wondering where you'll appear next. It was a mango tree last time,*' says the woman.

'*It's good to see you,*' says the old man. The woman smiles. Her eye catches something on the wall: two doll-like figures hanging near the ceiling.

'*I see you still have Inhumana and Grim,*' says the woman, nodding at them.

Hearing their names, the dolls turn their heads and grin at the woman.

The old man smiles. *'Yes. An innocent reminder of your childhood.'*

'They were troublesome. Always hungry for flesh,' says the woman.

'It's becoming increasingly difficult for them. Few people here venture out after dark any longer,' says the old man.

'Inhumana was unmanageably sadistic,' says the woman.

'I was proud of you. You taught her well except for her table manners, judging from what they say,' says the old man.

'They were messy eaters, just like me,' says the woman. *'I must be off now, Papa. After the tree, I become utterly famished. I, too, need flesh.'* The old man smiles benevolently.

Outside, the man is leaning on the car, waiting, his arms folded.

'Right, Vin, let's go,' says the woman as she unlocks the car. She starts the engine and pushes the accelerator to the floor, leaving a plume of dust behind them. It isn't long before they are back on the main road.

'You look so young. You look amazing. What's happened, Hoops?'

'Fruit is incredibly rejuvenating, Vin.'

'Obviously,' the man replies. 'You look so angelic.'

'Don't use that word. It gives me the shivers! Vin, may I ask you something? Do you like me?'

'Hoops, I have never liked anyone or anything so much.'

'Do you love me?' the woman asks.

Looking bewildered, the man hesitates. Whatever he's trying to say, he appears to be struggling. 'Hoops, I can't think clearly; I'm not certain what's happening to me. I care for you deeply, but I can't seem to say I love you. What's going on?'

'Relax, Vin. There's nothing to fret about.' The woman slams on the brakes, causing the tyres to squeal, and veers the car abruptly to the edge of the deserted road. She seizes the man and kisses him passionately.

'You taste so good, Vin.'

'Hoops, your tongue. It's so long, it's choking me.'

'It's not the half of it, Vin,' she whispers urgently in his ear. Her breath is hot and carries the scent of oranges and scorched earth as she tears into the man's flesh.

Angus Og

Gerry Webber

THOSE WHO KNEW HIM BEST called him Bragi or Ogma or sometimes Angus Og. So Angus it was upon which the townsfolk had settled, common people finding comfort in giving common names to things they do not understand.

Angus said little to anyone, though the Widow Martha, from whom he rented the cottage near the bridge, was thought to have heard him in the dead of night speaking in tongues with sprites or dwarves or grotesquely disfigured children, as her fancy, or the passage of the moon, dictated. But few believed her. Her hair was a restless sea of salty grey, and she was rumoured to have lost the balance of her mind after driving her husband insane with her endless wild imaginings. His body was never recovered, though Hamish the Butcher swore blind that he had found a piece of the old man's brain on the rocks below the cliff, which was all that was buried in the makeshift coffin over which Martha had been unable to weep. Or so it was said in the town.

Craigalister was a small town, little more than a village, and those who had lived there the longest, who occupied the larger houses set high above the river with featureless views of the churning sea, and feudal rights over the land above the cliffs, continued to insist that they were indeed Craigalister Villagers, chief amongst whom was The Laird, one of whose ancestors was reputed to have roped seven Jacobites to the back of a mare, which he cut with a jewelled blade and drove into the sea with a pack of hungry dogs. The Laird was blind in his right eye, which moved independently of his left, as if in search of a distant landmark or, according to some in the town, his only child, Catherine, who disappeared as a bairn.

And so it was that on a winter's night, as frost began to settle on the berries of the nearby yew tree, a stranger found his way to the inn and settled in the corner of the bar where at some point in the evening, accounts of which differ, the tall man, whose face was obscured by the shadow of his hood and whose lank beard reached to the centre of his chest, removed from its case a musical instrument the like of which none had seen before. Some said later that it was a kind of lute, or possibly a sort of viola, but others were adamant that it was a wind instrument of some description, and two of those who were sitting closest to the man, one of whom was the Butcher, spoke of it having a percussive quality akin to an African drum or the sound that a bone would make if rapped against a bleached skull. In any event, the rhythmic tune, the shape of which which no one could later recall, danced through the air to the furthest corners of the snug, where the Landlord was serving The Laird and keeping a watchful eye on the Widow Martha who, upon hearing the strange and ethereal sound, had closed her eyes and was swaying backwards and forwards in time to the music.

The Stranger, of course, was Bragi or Ogma or Angus Og, thereafter known as Angus.

———o———

Martha could not recall agreeing terms with Angus for the rental of the cottage, but there was much that she failed to remember. 'A deal's a deal,' she'd said to The Laird when he questioned her about the arrangement. He feared that the Stranger had taken advantage of the Widow, whose solitary lifestyle and weakness of mind made her, he thought, uniquely vulnerable to flattery and foolishness.

Consequently, it came as no surprise to The Laird to hear that the Widow had been seen coming and going from the cottage by the bridge under the cloak of darkness, nor to discover that the Stranger, Angus, had been heard playing shapeless tunes which drifted through the cold night air, hither and thither, like dandelion seeds on a summer breeze. Some described the music as sparse and tinny, like an old banjo being plucked in an empty church. Others spoke of xylophones and snare drums.

The Butcher took to his bed with a migraine that gripped the front of his head like a wrench, and blamed his illness on the relentless screeching of the Stranger's musical contraption, though none but he could remember hearing any such noise.

And then it happened, or so the townsfolk heard, but from whom they could not say. Perhaps it was the Postman who spread the word, or one of the delivery boys. Nobody knew. But the rumour spread throughout the town of Craigalister like a popular refrain, caught on the breeze in snatches of song: the Widow's husband was not dead after all. He had returned, from whence was unclear, and was living once again with his wife, Martha, though she would not let him leave the house for fear of losing him again, nor leave the house herself for fear that he would not be there when she got back. She had stopped drinking, and had tamed her wild widow-hair with the tortoiseshell brushes that her mother had given her as a wedding present. She had rediscovered the colourful clothes that she used to wear in years gone by. She was in love again. Enchanted. She was happy. She had no need of company. She had her husband back.

———— ○ ————

Receiving no answer when he rapped on the door of the Widow's house, The Laird decided to visit the Stranger at the cottage by the bridge. He was determined to discover the truth behind the rumours. Already, there was talk of sorcery and lunacy. Martha had not been seen for weeks, and he needed to be sure that the Stranger, Bragi or Ogma or Angus Og, whatever he called himself, was not holding the Widow captive in the cottage, and had not harmed her in any way, as he feared might be the case. It was his duty.

Angus opened the door before The Laird had been able to make himself known. 'I've been expecting you,' the Stranger said. 'Please, come in. I was just warming a pot of tea. Would you care to join me?' Unprepared for such a welcome, The Laird agreed, more from surprise than desire. He had visited the cottage once or twice before, but had rarely felt so much at ease with the place as he did now, against all his expectations. The main room into which he stepped was a sitting room with a kitchen at one end, or a kitchen that had space enough for sofas. It was warm and tidy with an aroma of freshly-shaved wood and oriental spice, though The Laird could see evidence of neither. There was a large window at the back of the cottage which overlooked the garden and the bridge beyond. The doors to the bedrooms were open. It was clear to The Laird that there was no one in the cottage save the Stranger.

The scene was unremarkable except for one thing. There in the corner was a musical instrument fashioned from metal and wood and ebony and brass and pipes and cloth and translucent hide and strings made from gut and slivers of ivory, the likes of which The Laird had never seen before. 'Let me play for you,' the Stranger said, handing The Laird a cup of tea the colour of rose hips in autumn. It carried the alluring aroma of nutmeg or cinnamon, or something else that The Laird could not at first, nor afterwards, identify.

And when the music was over and The Laird had left the cottage and returned to his house on the land above the river with featureless views of the churning sea, nothing of which the old man could remember, he went to bed and slept for two days as he calculated later, waking with a clear head and a steady eye to gaze beyond the grassy clifftops in search of wayward ships and breaching whales and kelpies and mermaids and distant landmarks, none of which were there to be seen.

But on the third day, as The Laird prepared to leave his house, there was a knock at the door, which the old man had not been expecting, and when at last he had grappled with the locks and bolts and pulled the heavy door ajar, he saw on the doorstep a young woman with long dark hair who reminded him for a moment of his darling wife, who many years ago had died of grief.

'Hello,' the woman said. 'My name is Catherine.'

———— ⊙ ————

The following day, a Saturday it must have been, Angus the Stranger took his customary seat in the corner of the tavern as the light outside was fading, and began quietly to play a popular melody the name of which regulars would later dispute. The snug was empty that night. Martha the Widow had become a recluse and The Laird was said to be unwell, or at any rate tearful and delirious. A woman, who was thought to be a private nurse, was tending to him in the family's ancestral home on the hill, so people understood, which was curiously full of light again, as it used to be in happier days, before The Laird's daughter had disappeared – snatched from the beach, folk said, though others, like the Butcher, had it that the parents killed the child and hid the body out of shame, which was why, he said, The Laird's wife took her life, though the death certificate said otherwise. 'Of course it did,' the Butcher said darkly.

The townsfolk in the bar were quiet too. Perhaps it was the time of year, or the thin purses that had followed the poor crop, but there was little laughter and less dancing than there normally was that evening, notwithstanding the lilt of the Stranger's music to which everyone was tapping their feet, though not in time with Angus, or each other.

And then, as if provoked, the Butcher burst through the door from the street and strode across the bar, shouting at the Stranger. 'I know what you're doing,' he yelled. 'I know what you're singing about, what you're saying about me.' The townsfolk in the bar stopped talking and looked at the Butcher. The Stranger never sang, they all agreed. Surely, the Butcher had gone mad. 'Stop it, man. I'm warning you!' the Butcher roared. 'One more word about me and the child and I'll swing f'ya. One more song about Martha's man and I'll rip you to shreds. See?' He brandished the knife that he used to slice mutton, and the men in the bar flinched as one. 'Folk around here know what happened, son. They don't need you and your deceitful songs.' The Stranger seemed oblivious to the commotion and continued to tease haunting melodies from the instrument before him – a crescendo of percussion as some remembered it, tranquil passages of woodwind others said, but all of them agreed: no song had been sung, no words had been spoken.

'No!' cried the Butcher. 'Not true, not true!' He clenched the handle of his knife and made as if to lunge for the Stranger, a blazing darkness in his eyes. But as he stepped forward, the knife fell to the floor and the Butcher clutched his head with both of his hands, consumed by unbearable pain. He fell to his knees and opened his mouth, as if to scream, but he made no sound, and the room fell silent. The Butcher appeared to have frozen, a grotesque statue in the middle of the bar, still kneeling upright, still with his hands to his head, still with his mouth agape. He glared at the shadow in the corner of the room, but his eyes were spent, as black holes to a tortured soul, deep and dark and empty.

And as the drama subsided, and the town's Doctor declared that the Butcher had died of a seizure, as fresh drinks were ordered, and conversations resumed, only then, when the Landlord called for music, did the townsfolk realise that the Stranger – Bragi, or Ogma, or Angus Og – had vanished.

The Terrible Trio

Chester Simpson

BERNARD PADDED GRUMPILY into the room, head down, tail straight, obviously in a mood. He sat by the sofa and stared accusingly at everyone. He'd been first to notice Sylvia was gone and had gone out looking for her. He'd followed her trail down to the harbour but then lost her scent. Back here in the flat, no one else seemed in the least concerned, it was as if Sylvia didn't even exist. At his mention of her name they threw him strange looks. It was baffling. Eventually, as the household retired to bed in ones and twos, he had no choice but to settle down for the night in Tilda's room.

By midnight, the house was in darkness. And quiet, though never completely silent, for the house creaked and groaned as it cooled. The night was a mild one. Bedroom windows, cracked open, ushered in the regular hoots and distant blares of foghorns on the river. These merged with the sounds of heavy breathing, occasional grunts and bouts of snoring coming from the first bedroom. Sometimes discordant but often in rhythm, it was like a small orchestra in muted repose, ticking over, biding its time. But in the very large bed in the second bedroom, only Patricia was asleep. The others tossed and turned, and lay awake, still worried…

Tilda (whispering): 'Pssst. Who is Sylvia?'

Gerda (whispering): 'Or rather, what is she?'

Bill Shakespeare (whispering): 'Fucked if I know.'

Bernard the Dog (looking at Patricia): 'What the Hell's happened to Patrick?'

Eventually sleep came to them all. Sometime later, the bedroom door creaked open and a small figure shuffled towards the bed.

'Mum, I can't sleep. I'm having nightmares. When will it be finished?'

'When will what be finished?' Tilda asked, instantly awake.

'The story the man is writing. Are we at the end yet?'

'No, son, not yet. One sleep from now and I'm sure he'll be finished then. So, Bernard,' Tilda put on her firmest, most commanding whisper, 'you have to get back to your own bed while Uncle Bill Shakespeare, Aunt Gerda and Uncle Patrick are here.'

'But Mum, the fog is scary. The man made it come, didn't he? I don't like his story. I want it to go away.' Bernard clambered over the snoring Bill Shakespeare and the lightly purring Gerda, and cuddled in beside his mother.

'OK, just this once,' Tilda said for the seventh night in a row.

'Why do you let him come in here every night?' Bernard the Dog protested. 'There's no room. He shouldn't have my name. He just confuses things, if you ask me.'

'Well, no one's asking you,' Tilda said. 'He's as much right to be called Bernard as you, and the man still hasn't figured what to rename you.'

'What!' Bernard yelled in his loudest whisper. 'I was here first. I was Bernard first. He's the one who should change, the little shit.' Bernard glowered at little Bernard who appeared to have fallen instantly asleep in the crook of his mother's arm.

'Well, you're a dog, and that's just the way it is.'

————o————

Through the night the fog cleared and the household woke to a bright sunny morning. The air was fresh and filled with birdsong. Bernard the Dog was first on the go, prowling from room to room, and made a couple of hopeful visits to the kitchen where his food bowl remained disappointingly empty. Far from blaming Tilda who normally attended to such things, he blamed the writer – whoever he was. Too busy working out how Bill Shakespeare will get his leg over Gerda, he supposed.

Gradually the house came to life. First up was Patricia who was sometimes a nurse at the local hospital and at other times was a gas repair man, but in either event would be first out of the house and off to work. Gerda was a primary school teacher and Clive a bus driver with Lothian Region Transport and would be next out. Fred and Robina worked with an insurance company in the city and would be last to leave. Bill Shakespeare was a writer and remained in bed. Tilda, as usual, was up early, preparing breakfast for little Arthur, who had finally settled in his own bed with his fluffy rabbit for company. She was Assistant Senior Editor with a book publishing company and was often able to work from home at least for part of the day. At 10.00 am the childminder Annalise arrived, enabling Tilda to get to her mid-morning planning meeting in the Grassmarket office.

She knew that today there should be plenty to discuss. So it proved. The agenda was a long one, and chairperson Rudi Dempster was anxious to set a brisk pace. His abrupt, no-nonsense style quickly accounted for the first four items up for consideration, but stalled frustratingly on item number five, the new collection of short stories by Ruaridh MacBlayne.

'His first novel was a hit,' conceded Pamela Strang, 'but his second was only a moderate success in terms of sales and didn't impress the critics. Then *Tramspotting*,' she rolled her eyes and shook her head. 'Topical, I suppose, but it bombed, and now we have these short stories. People don't buy short stories. I'm not sure about this collection at all.'

'Part of the problem is he never seems to know when he's finished. He submitted a late addition only yesterday.' Dempster checked his note pad. 'What was originally eight short stories is now eleven, and the third of them is practically a novelette.'

'Which one is that?' Tilda asked, suddenly suspicious.

'*Fog over Leith*,' Dempster said.

'I received an email from him first thing this morning,' Pamela Strang added. 'He wants to rename it *Who is Sylvia?*'

'This is becoming ridiculous.'

'I haven't seen that story yet – under either name,' Tilda said. 'But based on the rest of the collection, I think it's time we pulled the plug on Mr MacBlayne.'

'He has a loyal following,' Dempster reminded them. 'Five thousand sales guaranteed in hardback, probably another thirty thousand once it goes to paperback. The Independence lobby thinks he's a star, and laps up everything he does.'

'Funny thing is,' Pamela Strang mused, 'the *Fog over Leith* story reminded me so much of you, Tilda.'

'What do you mean?' Tilda asked, but with a sinking feeling that she knew very well what Pamela meant. The mystery author revealed.

'Well, you live in Leith...'

'As does anyone with taste.'

'...and your son is called Bernard, same as your dog...'

'My son is Arthur.'

'... and you live in this weird collective with an artist, a bus driver, a writer who hasn't written anything for three years, twins who always say the same thing at the same time, and this woman Patricia, or is it Patrick, who's neither one thing or another.'

'Well, never mind all that,' Dempster interrupted. 'Let's vote. Do we agree to publish MacBlayne or not? I, reluctantly, say Yea.' But both Tilda and Pamela Strang said nay, and that was it.

'I'll call his agent this afternoon,' Rudi Dempster said. The plug on Ruaridh MacBlayne was duly pulled.

Sitting on the number 22 bus that evening, headed towards the bottom of Leith Walk, Tilda's mind ran over the meeting again and again. Over lunch, she had read *Fog over Leith* for herself, and recognised everything in it. For Tilda, it was a simple decision. MacBlayne had to be stopped. She wondered how Scotland's most talked-about author would react to the news. Not well, it was safe to suppose. Tilda had come into contact with him on a few occasions, each of them a testament to the towering ego that was Ruaridh MacBlayne.

Stepping off the bus on Great Junction Street, then into the bakery to pick up a selection of pies and pasties for tonight's tea, Tilda saw that a mist was descending over Leith once again. By the time she was walking down Maritime Street the fog was dense, her steps along the narrow, cobbled street ringing out loud, echoing from the high walls of the one-time bonded warehouses crowding in on each side. There were few conventional doorways in the street. Instead, there were a number of wide openings, once upon a time large double-doored entrances to accommodate the wagons that hauled kegs of whisky and gin in and out. The doors were long gone, but, nowadays, each entrance led into a short, dark passage which opened out into a courtyard for car parking, and gave residents access to various combinations of modern flats, some four storeys high. All part of the New Leith. Usually, the view beyond the end of Maritime Street gave a limited view of the lights round the old harbour but not tonight, the lights were lost in the gloom that had descended.

MacBlayne is writing again, Tilda suddenly realised, and her stride quickened. She looked edgily over her shoulder at something moving behind her. A cat meowed loudly, darted across the street and disappeared into one of the old entrances. Tilda heaved a sigh of relief, laughed at her own foolishness, and rummaged in her large shoulder bag before entering the dark pend leading to her flat. As her hand closed round a bunch of keys she looked up at the slight sound and motion of a figure emerging from the shadows. He was tall, slimly built, unshaven, wearing a hooded jacket, a livid scar ran across his left cheek almost to the ear. She had never seen him before but Tilda knew instantly who this was – she had been reading about William Bauld, the lethal predator in *Fog over Leith*, only hours before. No surprise therefore to see the glint from the blade in his left hand, or the confident, almost gloating expression on his face as he bore down on her.

What did surprise her was the emergence of a second figure from the darkness and the equal look of shock on Bauld's face as he whirled round to meet him. He was too late. The second man, his face still in darkness, delivered a powerful swing with a baseball bat that caught Bauld full on the left side of the head above the ear. The crunch of hickory on skull was sickening, Bauld gave a grunt and collapsed, the switch-blade clattered on the cobbles. Tilda's saviour stepped into the light – it was Clive – and pulled his shoulders back to deliver a second blow, but Tilda leapt forward and grabbed his arm.

'No, Clive. That's enough. You may have killed him as it is.'

'Who is he? The bastard has been hanging around our entrance for the past half hour, obviously waiting for someone. I reckoned it had to be you – everyone else is back in the flat.'

'His name is William Bauld, he's a killer, but he doesn't really exist.'

The two stood over the fallen man, fascinated and horrified by the pool of blood that began to spread under his head and course across the pavement.

'He's bleeding a lot for man who doesn't exist,' Clive observed.

'Well, he exists in the world of Ruaridh MacBlayne,' Tilda said. 'The serial killer in *Fog over Leith* to be precise. It's MacBlayne who's behind all of this – the fog, Bernard's antics, Patricia's issues, everything.'

'So, what's he got against you?'

'Until today, probably nothing. Up to now, he's just been having a bit of fun at our expense. But this morning we cancelled his publishing contract. He's not the kind of man to take that with good grace. Clive, would you call an ambulance and the police? I've got to warn Pamela and Rudi Dempster. He could be going after all of us at Cowgate Publishing.'

'Well, not through him he won't,' Clive gestured at the prone figure. He did look extremely dead.

Tilda gave a bitter laugh. 'MacBlayne's got plenty of other shady characters like him. There's James Wardhaugh in *The Retro Man*, a sly, nasty piece of work, and the baby-faced killer Alfie Conn in *The Kipper Wars*. He's very proud of his villains, always calling them his 'Terrible Trio'.'

'Jeez!'

'But I've got a plan.' And with that Tilda grabbed her keys once more and hurried off to the flat.

———— ◦ ————

Bill Shakespeare's dry spell ran on and on. His last two works, both of them plays, one set in Denmark, the other in Verona, had been critical successes, both enjoyed extended runs at Stratford, but that was over two years ago. In any case, they had left him dissatisfied. Really, he yearned to get back to his Scottish roots, Tilda knew that all too well.

'I've got a new case for Ewen Macleod, if he's interested,' Tilda said to him.

'Oh? I haven't written about him for ages. I'd love to do that. A nice, juicy murder, I hope.'

'Not yet, as far as I know. But that's the point, to prevent a murder before it happens.' Tilda told him all about Ruaridh MacBlayne, and the incident with William Bauld out on the street. 'You have to get D.I. Macleod on the case – and I mean a.s.a.p.'

'How do I do that? You do realise he's fictional?' Bill Shakespeare gave her a strange look, but Tilda was unperturbed.

'Simpson's coffee buns,' she announced, producing a cake box from a carrier bag. 'That's Ruaridh MacBlayne's secret. I heard him on an Arts programme once talking about it. The interviewer praised the authenticity of his scenes and MacBlayne made a joke of it, saying it was down to coffee buns from Simpson the Baker. Nobody believed him of course, but then one day Rudi Dempster told me that MacBlayne admitted it at one of our launch parties when he'd had too much to drink. 'Authentic' and a bit more besides,' Tilda said bitterly.

'But MacBlayne is an old hand at this stuff. I've never done this sort of thing in my life. I wouldn't know where to begin.'

'Well, I *do* know where to begin,' Tilda gave him her most implacable look, and drew a large coffee bun from the cake box. 'And Bill, you're ten times the writer that clown will ever be.'

Tilda called Rudi's landline, then his mobile, but there was no answer. That worried her – Rudi was never more than ten feet from his phone. She called Pamela Strang who picked up immediately.

'Pam, it's Tilda. You OK?'

'Yes, why wouldn't I be?'

Tilda didn't speak. What a story – who would believe it?

'Tilda, are *you* OK?'

'Yes, I am. Pam, someone just tried to kill me outside my flat. I'm certain it's Ruaridh MacBlayne.'

'Ruaridh MacBlayne just tried to kill you. But you're all right.' Pam's voice dripped with scepticism. Tilda wasn't surprised.

'Not him personally but...someone paid by him. I'm fine. Clive stopped him. The man's lying outside, we think he's dead. The point is I'm certain MacBlayne has got people after all of us. I can't get an answer from Rudi.'

'That's unusual.' Pam sounded worried now.

'I've called the police. Pam, please be careful, don't go out, don't open the door to anyone, double-lock your doors, don't do anything you wouldn't normally do. Just lie low until tomorrow.'

'Well, I was just about to fix the wall socket in my bedroom...'

'Don't!' Tilda practically yelled. 'Don't do anything out of the ordinary.'

'Tilda, you sound really weird. I was about to say it's getting a bit too dark so I decided to fix it tomorrow...'

'DON'T! Don't mess with anything like that until we know what's happening.'

'All right, all right! You sound like my mother and she's a neurotic head-case.'

'Got to go, Pam. I think the police are here.'

———— ◦ ————

When the doorbell sounded, Ruaridh MacBlayne muttered grumpily and saved the work he had written, thought momentarily to close down the laptop but didn't, and headed for the door. He was pleased with how the story was progressing. William Bauld was in place and that bitch Tilda McEwan would get hers any minute now, he just needed to compose the end scene and - damn this interruption - he really couldn't wait to get back to it. This was his third – and final – draft. He already had the scene worked out in his head: how Bauld would stun her with a hard punch to the jaw, then, Tilda being an attractive woman, he would slash her from temple to jawbone, drag her into the shadows and cut her throat. Maybe he would gut her too. Yes, that would be a good touch but he'd have to think about the light needed for such work. Damn this interruption.

A good evening's writing, all the same. Alfie Conn had already taken care of Rudi Dempster. He had had it coming for some time and he wondered how long it would take the police to find the gay twat in the river, complete with his new cement boots. Maybe never.

He was almost out of coffee buns, just one left, but that would be enough to deal with Tilda, so MacBlayne wasn't worried. He'd get more from the bakery in the morning. By the time they found Tilda McEwan, realised Dempster was missing, and put two and two together, it would be too late to save Pamela Strang anyway. He sort of liked Pamela and her end would be the cleanest of the three. Women and electricity, never a good combination. Trying to fix a dodgy light switch, she wouldn't know much about it. Not a bad way for any of us to go, MacBlayne reflected. He sighed and opened the door.

Two uniformed police officers with impassive expressions flanked a man in plain clothes, who spoke now.

'Mr MacBlayne? Mr Ruaridh MacBlayne?'

'Yes.'

'My name's Detective Inspector Ewen Macleod. These are officers Turnbull and Stanton from the Leith Constabulary. May we come in for a moment, sir? We just have a few questions we'd like to clear up.'

'Why... why, yes, I suppose so,' MacBlayne said, unwilling to invite them in, unable to think of a plausible reason not to. As they entered the living room, MacBlayne saw the white screen of his laptop and made a casual move to step round one of the police officers and close the session. But the officer stepped directly into MacBlayne's path. Instead, DI Macleod walked round the other side of the desk and stared at the screen.

'As Tilda McEwan rummaged in her large shoulder bag for her door keys,' he read out loud, *'William Bauld stepped from the shadows, a look of triumphant expectation on his face. Slashing and gutting her would feel good, no question, but for Bauld the best time always came before. Right now, in fact, with the first delicious moment of fear, the first realisation by the victim that whatever was about to happen to her, it was going to be very bad indeed, and that there was no escape.'*

'Oh dear, Mr MacBlayne. Pretty crap writing, if I may say so, but I think we can forego the questions here, and go straight to Stage Two.'

DI Macleod somehow seemed to add two extra inches to his height, and said, 'Ruaridh MacBlayne, you are under arrest for the attempted murder of Tilda McEwan and for the possible abduction and murder of Mr Rudi Dempster. At this point, anything you say may be taken down and used in evidence against you.'

'You can't do this!' MacBlayne exploded. 'Who do you think you are? This isn't in the fucking script!'

DI Macleod smiled, 'It is in mine, Sonny Jim, it is in mine.'

Alone

Lesley Henderson

NEEDLES SLICE AT MY FACE as I battle my way through the snow and wind. The coldness is seeping in to my bones, my body shivering and shaking. These are not my clothes and they are not keeping me dry or warm. I saw the weather forecast on the television this morning in the TV room and had not expected this. The temperature on the chart was marked as -2°C and the picture showed sunshine and snow showers. At home in Antalya it regularly can be down to -7°C in the winter but this feels so much colder than that.

I stop abruptly, causing someone to bump into me. I murmur sorry but they grunt in reply and walk on. I am wondering whether just to go back but I know I need to do this, so I trudge on up the hill to where the lady in the hostel told me there is a library. I have been sitting for the last few days in the hostel staring at the walls trying to work up the energy to go out. I push my wet and numb feet forward one at a time slithering inside these ill-fitting shoes. At the top there are traffic lights and the wind howls around. I have been told that Edinburgh is a beautiful city but at the moment, in these blizzard conditions, I can see nothing.

My instructions are to cross the road then cross again. I climb the steps into an old building and a welcome blast of hot air envelops me. I see a queue at the desk and I join it. The woman looks at me and my clothes. I recognise that look. It is the same look that I used to give. I suddenly feel ashamed of my previous self, so certain that I was right, just as she is now. She begins firing questions at me, her words too fast for me to understand. I shrug and shake my head. She sighs and holds up a card. I shake my head. She then points to a sign on the wall. I can make out a few words. 'Do not deface books', 'No eating', 'No sleeping'. She glowers at me while still speaking fast in a loud voice, as if I am hard of hearing, but she opens the gate and lets me in.

I turn back intending to ask where the language sections are but she is already speaking to another person. I know, without understanding the words, that she is complaining about me. I feel my shoulders slump and try to remind myself that I am an intelligent woman, but the events of the last few months have taken their toll. The librarian had reminded me of some of the unhelpful staff in the detention centre, and the feeling of powerlessness overwhelms me again.

I start to walk up the aisles happy at least to be in the warm. I can see there are others, of all ages, like me in mismatched, poorly fitting clothes sitting at desks, some clearly struggling to stay awake. A woman smiles at me and nods her head in the direction of the librarian.

'She's a crabbit one, pay her no heed hen.'

I have no idea what the woman is saying but I guess that she is sympathising with me, and I feel extraordinarily grateful and smile warmly at her. As I wander around I wonder about their stories, what had happened to them. I vow to myself that I will not make snap judgements in future, hoping that my recent experiences will help me stick to that. I eventually find a section with books on *Teach Yourself Turkish* and English/Turkish dictionaries. I am relieved that I remembered to bring the paper and pen the woman at the hostel gave me. She gave me a map and told me the bus number through gestures and counting on her fingers. Luckily, it was a number 10 bus. She was so kind, not like the woman on duty the day I arrived.

That woman had quickly shown me to my room, on the way waving her hand at doors barking out words I did not understand, they didn't even sound like English. She had grabbed sheets from a cupboard and dumped them in my arms. She knocked on my door and barged in a few minutes later with a box of groceries and cleaning materials and marched back out again.

Her parting words were, 'After this ye get yer own messages.'

I puzzled over that for a long time wondering if it meant I was not allowed to receive post. No one knew where I was so I decided that this was not relevant to me. Later, another resident told me that she was a 'nippy sweetie' and not to worry. I wasn't sure what she meant, but I understood that it was not a compliment and she helpfully showed me the 'TV room' and 'laundry room'.

I find a seat near a heater and start to flick through the dictionary feeling homesick as I do so. I gathered from the unpleasant librarian that I could not take out books as I didn't have a card. I urgently need to find a bookshop and hope that I can afford to buy a dictionary. How I miss my Apple phone and my laptop. Like most people, if I wanted to say something in a different language I just used Google translate. I have been trying to teach myself English since I arrived but I find it really hard. Since arriving in Scotland I am finding it almost impossible to understand people. I jot down the phrases I am going to need today as well as a few other words I think might be helpful. Once my feet and hands have thawed out, I leave.

It is just as cold and snowy when I get back outside, but this time at least the wind is behind me. I head back the way I came as I knew that was where I was to get the bus. At the bottom of the hill I notice that there are lots of shops on the other side of the road. I hadn't noticed them before as I was focused on following my directions. I cross over and spot a bookshop. I relax as I enter. It reminds me of my favourite bookshop in the street near my flat.

I go up to the desk feeling more confident and read out what I had written.

'Hello kind sir, you me help please. I am wanting dictionary for Turkish to English read.'

The man looks blankly at me and stretches out his hand towards me. I am momentarily confused, then remember that it is an English custom to shake hands. I take his hand and shake it. He grabs his hand back and laughs shaking his head and pointing to my note. I immediately realise my error and hand it to him, my face burning as I look away. I realise he is speaking to me and I reluctantly raise my eyes. His eyes are kind and he gestures for me to follow him. He shows me several English to Turkish dictionaries and some English to Turkish phrase books which I think I can use back to front. I am delighted.

'Thank you. Thank you.'

'*Rica ederim,* you are welcome!'

I smile stupidly and laugh and nod at him, feeling overwhelmed by his kindness. I suddenly have an image of the nodding dog my dad used to have in his car making me smile even more. As I turn towards the shelves another image comes to my mind, and my eyes fill with tears remembering the car bomb that took my parents from me. I try to concentrate on choosing a book and working out whether I can get one or two. I look again at the coins and few notes in my pocket. I never used to carry money, I always just relied on paying by card but my accounts have been frozen. No, I will not allow the tears to come again. I make myself focus on the task and settle on a mini dictionary and a phrase book which will at least give me something to do when I get back.

I think of the awful room that is now my home. The bare walls, the peeling paint, sleeping, eating and cooking in the one room. Sitting staring at these walls, I had to try not to think of my beautiful apartment in the old part of Antalya overlooking the river. I did not appreciate how lucky I was, I don't suppose anyone appreciates what they have until they no longer have it. It is not the lack of home comforts that is the hardest to bear. It is the loneliness and emptiness I feel from the moment I wake till the time I finally fall into a fitful sleep. I miss my aunts, my cousins, my friends and my colleagues. I miss who I was, the whole familiar routine of my life.

Yet, despite the weather I do feel better being out of the room. Yesterday I felt as if I was disappearing, as if I no longer existed. I am embarrassed to remember that I walked around the room touching the walls, touching the grubby carpet, patting and pinching my arms, pulling my hair trying to feel something. The room does not even have a mirror. Maybe I could buy a small one today. The thought cheers and mocks me at the same time.

I return to the cash desk but it is a different assistant who takes my money, I think she is now asking me if want a bag. I am confused why would I not want a bag? The girl holds up a plastic bag and I nod, so much nodding. Next door to the book shop is what looks like a chemist. This feels safer to me, large and anonymous, and I successfully purchase a small mirror without any words being exchanged.

My next challenge is to find the right bus stop and I am so pleased with myself when I find it without too much difficulty, but the display indicates it will be another 35 minutes before my bus. So I decide to go and get myself a coffee at the cafe I just passed. At the counter the young man asks me something so quickly that I can't understand him. I assume he is asking what I want so I ask for coffee. He shakes his head in irritation and points to different size cups. I point to the smallest. Then he is asking me something else. I think he is asking if I want milk so I nod again. I hand over some of the coins but he shakes his head and rolls his eyes, so I get more coins out of my pocket. Still not enough. A woman next to me says something and then he is moving me on, pointing to where you collect the coffee. I am confused but then realise that the woman must have paid for my coffee. I turn back to thank her but she stares at me coldly so I just nod again and smile. The woman is smartly dressed and waiting impatiently for her takeaway coffee so that she can return to her busy important life. A sigh escapes my lips.

I return to the bus stop and an older woman who reminds me of my aunt starts to speak to me. I nod and smile but only make out a few of her words. She is saying something that sounds like 'Granweans, Australia' and shows me photos of children on her phone. I think these must be her grandchildren. Although I only understand a little of what she is saying, I can feel and identify with her sense of loss and loneliness. As she gets on her bus she gives me an unexpected quick hug saying, 'I do like a guid blether.'

I look up this word in my dictionary when I get on the bus but it's not there. Oh well. I start to think about my aunt and wonder how she is, missing her familiar and comforting face. I have not allowed myself to dwell on the day six months ago that my life changed. It started as a day like any other. As usual I was busy rushing from one clinic to another. I was mulling over the topic of my next lecture. I knew I had been careless with the content of my last lecture. No one knew about my involvement with the movement and I needed to keep it that way, as since 2016 anybody dissenting could be in danger.

I was just entering the hospital ward when my phone vibrated. A few minutes later and I would not have heard it with the noise in the ward. As I read the message I felt as if a hand was squeezing my heart. I tried to take a deep breath but choked. I dithered trying to decide whether to go back or continue to do the ward round. The decision was made for me as my registrar appeared at the door of the ward, and my feet automatically walked through the door. I completed the ward round on autopilot, trying not to seem too distracted, thoughts racing round my head. I walked purposefully back to my office, not allowing myself to break into a run, mentally going over the list of what I needed to do. I ditched my white coat, gathered up the few papers that connected me to the movement – I would put them in the confidential waste as I left. I retrieved both my passports as well as my CV and qualifications from their hiding place. I wrote a short note to my employer explaining I had been offered a new job abroad, keeping it vague and apologising for the inconvenience, but noting that I had not taken any holidays in almost a year. The letter would not be found until after the weekend. I picked up my handbag and gym bag, disposed of the papers and left. I walked quickly in the direction of the gym but kept walking, flagging down a taxi, resisting the urge to look behind me.

At the airport the first plane to depart was to London. I booked a ticket at the desk, paying in cash as instructed. The next two hours before the plane departed were the longest of my life. Just as boarding started I sent two text messages, one to my aunt and one to my best friend, saying that I had been offered my dream job abroad and at the last minute had decided to accept. I told them that once I was settled I would get in touch with them. I knew they wouldn't believe me, but hopefully it would convince the authorities they were not involved and it would buy my friends in the movement time. I then removed the sim, and dumped it and my phone in separate bins. I only started to relax a little once I was in the air. That though was when the enormity of what I was doing started to hit me. I hoped and prayed that my family and friends would not get into trouble.

Back at the hostel the woman at the desk gives me a letter. I am terrified to open it. I know no one in this city. Using my dictionary I understand that I have an appointment tomorrow to see a lawyer. I go back and show the woman at the desk to ask her how to get there, but she gestures to me that I can walk – it is only 15 minutes – she shows me on the map she gave me earlier. I cannot sleep that night worrying about what this means.

I find the office quite easily and arrive early. A young woman beckons me into her office. An interpreter stands up and makes introductions. I am asked to explain what led me here. This is the first time since arriving six months ago that I have been asked this question. Previously I was just asked for proof of who I was. I had been told to say I was seeking asylum for political reasons and they did not ask me more. I begin to speak hesitantly at first and then more confidently. I tell my story as neutrally as I can, enjoying speaking in Turkish.

The young woman gives no sign as to whether she believes me or not, but makes notes and then asks me some questions clarifying certain points, for example, exactly what my role was in the movement, how long I had been involved and so on. My voice breaking I also told her what had happened to my parents.

'You are fortunate,' she says, 'the UK government is now recognising political asylum seekers from Turkey. They have acknowledged that the imprisonment and torture of opponents of the regime is an evidenced fact. However,' she pauses, 'that does not mean you will automatically be given the right to remain, but you do seem to fit the Home Office's own criteria.'

I feel a weight fall off my shoulders hearing this, and ask her what probably everyone asks.

'How long will this take?'

With a shake of her head she explains she is not able to give me any idea of timescale. She reassures me that she will do her best to move the process on as quickly as possible, but to prepare for it to take a minimum of several months and most likely a lot longer. I am glad she is being honest with me. As I make for the door she calls me back and gives me a note with an address on it. She explains that this is an organisation that helps asylum seekers and puts them in touch with others. They can also help with practical things like language classes and so on. I give her a grateful nod.

As I walk back to the hostel I feel, for the first time since I arrived in this country, that leaving Turkey was the right thing to do and maybe someday life will get better again. That sets me thinking again about who had betrayed me but I know thinking that way will lead me to a dark place. I have been telling myself over and over that I am one of the lucky ones – I hadn't been arrested or tortured and as far as I know none of my remaining family have been arrested. I remind myself that I have escaped. I am lucky to be here, lucky to be alive.

At the hostel, some kind of party is going on. The kind woman gestures for me to go through into the TV room. A meal of some kind is being served and a man is reciting what sounds like a poem in a language I do not recognise. The woman quietly says it is 'Burns Night' and motions me over to a table where I am served unrecognisable food. 'It's haggis, neeps and tatties, it'll put hairs on yer chest,' the woman serving says jokingly so I think she doesn't really mean it. I have absolutely no idea what the food is. I look for a seat and a woman points to the seat beside her. A man says something to the woman but she tells him, 'Haud yer wheesht, she's sitting here.' The man laughs in a good-natured way and gestures me over. People turn and smile at me as I sit listening to the strange words in the company of strangers, eating the strange but tasty hot and filling food, no longer feeling quite so alone.

Taste in Friends

Norma Hurley

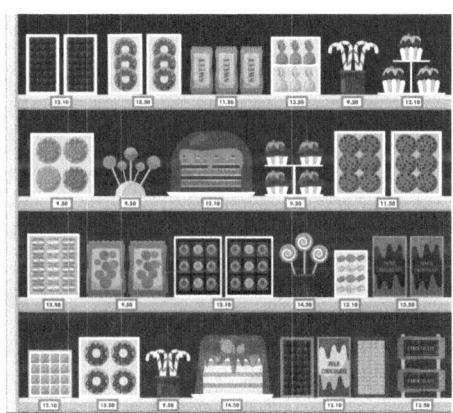

S HE TREATED PEOPLE LIKE SWEETIES.

Some she treated like the expensive, hand-made chocolates she would occasionally enjoy. She had a routine. She would start slowly, scanning the pictures and descriptions of the chocolates on the card, allowing herself time to feel which particular delicacy suited her mood. She would select one and place it carefully in her mouth, allowing her tongue to lick at the surface, rolling it around her palate, the warm saliva mixing with the melting chocolate to form a liquid of pure and intense pleasure, then sucking or biting into the hidden joy that lay within.

In the same manner, on occasion, depending on her mood, she would select one or two of her very special friends – discreet, highly intelligent, highly sophisticated, cultured men and women – and invite them to the latest hit at the theatre, or a light supper in a newly discovered on-trend restaurant, or to the private view of an up-and-coming young artist's work.

With her boxes of Charbonnel et Walker or Godiva, she disciplined herself against over-indulging in something she knew she might enjoy a little too much. And then regret.

So with these friendships. They were her very private treats, not to be shared widely or lightly, or frequently. She luxuriated in the company of these friends, even if sometimes, despite her well-honed skills of social intercourse, she returned home at the end of an evening feeling a little too sated with the rich and velvety coating of their intimacies.

She was what is often called a self-made woman, although she would scoff at the idea. *Are we not all self-made?* she would ask, raising an eyebrow in ridicule. It just so happened she had made a better fist of making herself than most.

She had risen from a council house and comprehensive school in Renfrewshire, where not too much was expected of her, to become rich, powerful, and influential, with a penthouse in Canary Wharf. This was partly because of the luck which to some degree accompanies all success. It was also due to the accident of intelligence, and the advantage of an attractive face. But mostly, her status and wealth were the result of hard work, determination, ambition, and ruthlessness.

She shunned the limelight. She preferred to work in the shadows, nudging government policy here, where it could improve her clients' fortunes, negotiating deals with foreign leaders on behalf of private interests, acting as the go-to go-between between financiers and industrialists. She worked for super-wealthy individuals and conglomerates who trusted her and her discretion, and who rewarded her handsomely.

Some of her clients became her very special friends. She cultivated them carefully, mixing those who might benefit from the interaction, maintaining distance amongst those whose tastes and interests differed.

She was single by choice, but not celibate. Her taste in men was catholic and eclectic, and her appetite for sex voracious. Relationships seldom lasted but that suited her. She had friends. She did not need a man clinging to her.

Indeed, she had other friends, older friends, from school and university, whom she treated like the mixed bags of boilings she also loved, the favourites from her childhood. They were her alter ego, her release.

Unlike her passion for chocolate, she was less precious and more roughly carnal about her intake of these sweet treats. She enjoyed the exquisiteness of the unknown, the moment of anticipation as she dipped her hand into the paper bag, the slight sweat on her fingertips seeking out the sticky surface of the sweet. Would it be a soor ploom, a Berwick cockle, a sherbet lemon, or a treacle toffee that she plucked out?

She took open pleasure in throwing the catch into her mouth, the immediate taste, the satisfaction of sucking then crunching down on the hard confection, the after-taste, the lingering sweetness or sweet-sourness of remembrance. She would dip her hand in again, seeking the next experience.

And then later, in her bathroom, she would run her tongue over the cloying film of sugar that coated her mouth, and scrub her teeth clean and her gums raw with her toothbrush.

These friends were a less exclusive set, from different classes and backgrounds, not all professionals, or even particularly well-educated.

She understood them well. As with her special friends, she would bring them into her orbit by selecting a varied range of individuals, encouraging a coming together of interests, attractions, of mutual endeavours – connections which they would often only discover they had after she had introduced these friends to each other.

Now and again she held dinner parties for this less elite group of friends, great raucous affairs, guests made flushed and fluent by good wine and delicious food.

She liked to observe their coming together, their transactions, and their continuing contact with each other. She felt, if not in control, then at least an influence over what happened to these friends, but she didn't feel they had to be central to her life. If and when they tired her she replaced them with others. Sometimes temporarily, sometimes permanently. There were always plenty of individuals to choose from. Relationships were fluid, transient, transitory. That was how she preferred it.

Of course she maintained a separation between the two groups of friends. They offered her different things. They were different one from another. They would not get on. And besides, she was not sure she wanted them to.

Then it happened. It was not of her making, nor of her choice. Nor was it deliberate, it couldn't have been.

The disaster, for that is what it was – a dreadful, gut-wrenching, humiliating disaster – was not intended or deliberate, or was it?

Surely not. It didn't seem so at the time. No, it was done from the best of intentions, wasn't it?

It was a special occasion, a birthday with a nought on the end. She had quite deliberately arranged nothing for her birthday. It was not an age to celebrate. It was not an age she wanted everyone in her circle to know she had reached. She would take a week off work and go to India on her own. Do some yoga, relax, think about what the next decade might bring.

She told her plans to her two oldest university friends from back in her Glasgow days. They would know her birthday and might expect her to do something, have an event. She was quite specific – no fuss, no presents. She saw they were disappointed. But well, it was time she thought of herself for a change.

Her flight to Kerala was on the Saturday afternoon. Reluctantly, under pressure from the university friends, she agreed to birthday cocktails on the Friday evening. It was arranged for an extremely smart hotel – one she usually frequented with her other, special set of friends. Disconcerting but not dangerously so. It would be a fleeting visit.

They were sitting in a booth in the cocktail lounge, on their second round of espresso martinis. She was beginning to relax. She didn't see the men approach.

'Well, for God's sake, who do we have here? What a surprise! I'd heard you were abroad.'

One of her clients – a real estate developer, important and influential – and another man whom she didn't recognise, stood in front of her. She had last seen her client leaving her hotel bedroom in Dubai in the early hours around a month previously. It had been a one-off. He was fun but no more than that. And married. Of course.

She smiled, her pulse racing:

'Tomorrow. India. This is a surprise – what are you doing here?'

'Off to a fucking boring dinner in the restaurant with a bunch of Goldman Sachs investment managers. Bloody banker wankers. Just thought we'd drop in for a snifter first.'

From the slur in his voice she thought he'd already had more than one snifter.

'What are you girls up to – celebrating something?'

Without waiting for a reply he turned his expensively created smile on her two friends.

'Shall we just join you for a quick one?'

He moved to sit down as his companion went to order drinks at the bar.

'Introduce us then – not often we get a chance to sit with three beautiful women in one place.'

'Creep,' murmured one of the university friends. Introductions were made.

The second man reappeared, followed by a waiter bearing a bottle of champagne and five glasses. He set them down on the table and poured the drinks.

The second man raised his glass towards the three women.

'Well, cheers. Are you girls working tonight?'

'Working? – oh no, night off for us.' One of the university friends smiled at him and raised her glass in return.

'Didn't think I'd seen you in here before. Don't you usually work the Grosvenor?'

'There or the Dorchester,' the second university friend replied.

'Ah, yes, that's where. I knew we'd met before. Well, nothing like a busman's holiday I suppose.' The man laughed at his own wit. He turned to the birthday girl. 'But not seen you before. Are you at the Dorchester too?'

She felt the blood rising in her cheeks. She looked at her client. He was looking at her. Silently. Quizzically. Amused.

She looked at her friends. They smiled at her. In fact they were trying to smother their giggles. Their expressions read: *Didn't you know? Did you really not know what we do?*

Then it hit her.

They were 'working girls'. Bloody high-class call girls, working out of the best hotels in London.

No, she had not fucking well known. She had thought they did something in the city. Like her, she had thought. But of course, something more menial.

The men downed their glasses and stood up to leave.

Her client pulled her to him and whispered in her ear.

'Well, I suppose I was lucky. I didn't have to pay for it.'

He walked away, his arm slung around his companion's shoulder. She could hear the roar of their laughter as he finished telling him his story.

She stood and lifted her coat and bag.

'How could you do this to me?'

Her friends looked at one another. Hurt expressions on their faces.

'We thought you knew, we really did.'

She walked off. Feeling the hot sting of tears on her cheeks. Tasting the bile of champagne in her mouth.

Heroes of Our Time

Liz Logie MacIver

THE BUS WAS DUE IN THREE MINUTES according to the app on her phone. Debbie considered the day ahead. Three appointments. Three clients. She climbed onto the No. 27 clutching her pass.

The bus was packed. She managed to squeeze into a seat on the top deck next to a large woman with inky-blue tattoos depicting exotic birds on her forearms. The woman was probably quite young. It was pretty hard to tell what her bone structure was as her face and body were concealed by pillows of fat. There was a vague smell of fried food and shower gel pervading the top deck. The 27 headed over the Mound and most of the passengers got off in town.

A young man sat down in front of Debbie accompanied by a middle-aged woman with thinning hair. Her unkempt hair was coloured in three different hues of red. There was a strong sense of alcohol or maybe cheap perfume. She recognised the relationship between them. As they headed down Pennywell Road near where she would get off, the young man asked the woman what she was going to buy at the supermarket.

'Not sure, son. But I need toilet paper and fags, that's for sure,' she muttered.

Debbie got off the bus outside Gerry's café. She checked her watch: 9.45. Time to get a coffee? Probably not. She put her work mobile on. No messages. The street was narrow and the tenements tightly packed on each side. She pushed open the main door with peeling green paint. The bells had ceased to function a long time ago. First floor right. There it was again, that sweet-and-sour odour of urine in the stairwell as she arrived at the door. She knocked loudly. She wondered if he might be asleep. A few seconds passed, and then the door opened slowly.

'Hi there, Kevin. How are you today?' Debbie started brightly.

A young man stood in front of her. He wore a grubby white tee shirt with 'Lamb of God' written across it and the crucifixion depicted in the centre. There were several brown stains on the sides and bottom of the shirt. Tea stains, Debbie hoped. Kevin didn't reply to her greeting but opened the door to let her in.

The smell hit her immediately she entered. Indeterminable. The living room was small with a bay window. It was dark, so Debbie opened the curtains. The floor was covered in books. There were no pictures on the walls.

'So, what would you like to do today?' Debbie sounded upbeat.

Kevin rolled a cigarette and stared at her. He had very green eyes. Small and piercing. His wiry black beard was curly and unkempt.

'Do you want me to clean your sink? It looks like it might need it,' Debbie suggested.

He lay down on a brown sofa at the window and closed his eyes.

Kevin grunted. 'Yep, whatever…'

'OK then, that's a good start. How have you been feeling this week?'

'The same, you know. What's the point?' Kevin didn't open his eyes.

Debbie checked under the sink in the small galley kitchen for a cloth. There was a brown-and-green-stained J-cloth. She rinsed it under the tap and wished she had rubber gloves as she surveyed the sink. The steel sink was encrusted with old food and larger mounds of soft brown matter. There was a terrible stench from the drain. She felt like gagging but knew this was impossible, so she thought of the green park with sweet-smelling flowers near her house to deflect from her urge to throw up.

'So, did you think about my suggestion to get out and take a walk every day?'

'Nope. We are all gonna die anyway, so what would the point be in that?'

'Well, it might help, you know.' Debbie was concentrating very hard on a particularly thick piece of gunge which was stuck to the side of the sink. She took out a kitchen knife and started to hack away at it.

'What would you like to talk about today, Kevin?'

'Eh… what about yon army guys? I read about that terrorist on the Amsterdam train. Good job they were there. Heroes, eh? Heroes for a day.'

Kevin was brightening up a bit. He was going to light up a cigarette but had second thoughts. He was not supposed to smoke when she was there.

Debbie finished the sink. She washed her hands under the tap for several minutes.

'Do you want a cuppie tea, hen?' Kevin asked.

'Yes, OK, I'll make it. Do you want one?'

'Ta, that'll be grand.'

Debbie lifted up the kettle and filled it. The cups looked really dodgy. Either cracked or dark brown inside. She only made one cup for Kevin.

'I think I will pass on the tea. I had one about an hour ago,' she lied.

The fridge was empty apart from a shrivelled-up apple and some sour milk.

'Is it OK without milk?'

'Yeah, I suppose so. I'll need to get some.'

'I will pop down and get a pint before I go,' Debbie smiled.

'So, what were we sayin'?' Kevin leant over and picked up his mug.

'These army guys on the train… who were on holiday, but by good luck were on the train when the guy with the Kalashnikov got on,' Debbie reminded him.

'Yeah, these guys were stars right enough, eh? They do a great job. Helpin' with the migrants too. They are my idea of heroes.' Kevin slurped his tea loudly.

He carried on talking.

'I read about the heroes in Ancient Greece but they are just characters in an ancient story....'

Debbie leaned forward and smiled at Kevin.

'You are right about these guys on the train. There was a blaze of publicity – heroes in a moment, but forgotten soon after. Not many heroes that last nowadays. Greece had its heroes but that poor country is struggling,' Debbie reflected.

'So, forgotten heroes again, then?' Kevin affirmed.

'Do you read the papers often, Kevin? And some books, I see?' Debbie picked up a copy of *War and Peace* from the pile strewn on the floor.

'Yeah, I read a lot. I wanted to be a teacher.'

'You could still do that, Kevin.'

'Not until I am better. People don't understand.'

The bedroom door was open and Debbie caught sight of something glistening on top of the bed.

'Do you want me to clean in the bedroom today?'

'No, I would rather chat. You can borrow *War and Peace* if you want?'

'Thanks, but I have a copy. What's that on your bed?'

'Go and have a look.' Kevin pointed at the door.

Debbie pushed the door open. There was a tent on top of the unmade bed. The whole tent was covered in tinfoil.

'Why have you covered your tent in tinfoil and set it up on the bed, Kevin?' Debbie knew the answer but wanted to hear him say it.

'It's to stop me hearing them.' Kevin rubbed his brow vigorously.

'Who are *they*?' Debbie asked, staring at the tent.

'The voices... they come on the radio and I hear them at night. The foil protects me.'

'You're taking your medication every day, though?'

'Yeah, yeah, no sweat.'

'That's good that you are safe in the tent, then?' Debbie looked at Kevin to reassure him.

'So, do you live near here?' Kevin deflected. 'Or in a posh part?' Debbie smiled.

'I come by bus if that's what you mean?'

'No, but where do you come from?'

'The south side.'

'The tourists don't know the half of it, eh?' Kevin declared.

'You're right, Kevin. Edinburgh is a city that has two sides.'

'Us folk in poorer parts, hidden away.'

'Can I help out with anything else?' Debbie sneaked a look at her watch.

'I think the toilet is on the blink again.'

Debbie went through to the toilet room next to the bathroom. The bowl was full of paper and smeared with faeces. The stench caught her throat and she coughed. She opened the tiny cracked window to let in some air and filled a bucket with water from the sink.

'God, Kevin, how long has it not been flushing?'

'Weeks now. I need to put some water down to clear it.'

'You need to get a plumber to look at it soon.'

'What's the point? It costs too much and the bucket works.'

'That's our time up now but I will pop down and get that milk for you.' Debbie made a mental note to report the toilet problem.

'Ta for that.' He handed Debbie a pound coin.

As Debbie came out into the air, her work mobile was ringing. It was the office. She had to ring in regularly after each visit so that they knew she had left the client.

' You OK, Debs?' a familiar voice spoke.

'Yeah, just took longer with Kevin than I thought. Getting him some milk.'

'Your police check is through. They just need your build. I said medium?'

'Yes, I am medium build.'

'Great, see you at the office later. Bye, Debs.'

Debbie bought some milk and a hand sanitiser at the corner shop. She popped back and put the milk in Kevin's fridge.

'See you next week then, Kevin?'

'Yeah, maybe eh?'

Debbie headed to Gerry's café. She was meeting the next client there. A woman with alcohol problems. Debbie was facing her next challenge of the day. This poor client was confronting demons from her past and fighting against her addiction. She hoped this client would turn up, as she was often unreliable.

She squeezed a little of the clear antibacterial liquid into her hands. She felt guilty, somehow.

Anyway, the day was going well so far, and Kevin seemed happier. She was ready for her next challenge, her everyday routine.

Old Spice Was Always With Me

Judith Wall

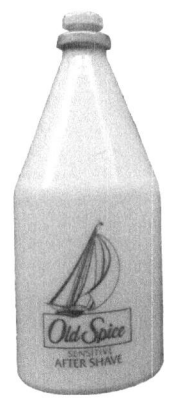

Tuesday 9ᵗʰ May, 1989.

I tell you I could smell it as soon as I got inside the flat: Old Spice, the fragrance of the '60s. It gave me a shock, a real weak-kneed shock, as I lived on my own. An old couple lived upstairs and Miss Brown, a retired librarian, was downstairs. My flat was the smallest of the three, sort of squashed in at the mezzanine level. Entering through the door at the turn of the stairs, you turned right down a small hall. Facing you at the end was the bathroom, squashed between a combined living room and kitchen to the left, and a bedroom to the right. I stepped back on to the stairs, sniffing, but couldn't smell anything out there. I went in and shut the door. You'll think I'm daft, but I sniffed round the letterbox to make sure that nobody had poured some aftershave lotion through it. I went into the living room and opened the window to sniff outside but there was no smell out there. I did the same in the bathroom and bedroom, but there was nothing.

It was lucky that I'd bought fish for tea, so the smell of it soon masked the aftershave lotion. I felt a bit upset as I was eating it. I couldn't help thinking about the old days, you see. I didn't usually let myself dwell on the past, but that scent had taken me right back to the time before my parents died in a car crash. I was born in 1955, and by '65 I was an orphan. I'm not saying that to make you feel sorry for me, but somehow it's the smells that take me back and make me feel weepy. I always associate Mum with the smell of baking, and Dad with Old Spice.

Well, you can see why it had upset me. Anyway, I allowed myself to remember the good old days for a few minutes, and then turned my mind to what I should wear to go down to the pub with my old school friends. Jane was bringing some guy she'd been seeing for a few weeks. She said he was keen to meet her friends, and she obviously wanted to show him off. I called for Lisa and Jill and we all went down together.

Oh, God! I saw them as soon as I got through the door, and my heart sank like a sack of potatoes. She was with this creep who I'd met at a party a few weeks ago. I mean, slimy doesn't begin to describe him. He was one of those weird people who take it as a personal insult if you just have one dance with them and then say, 'Thank you.' I'd only danced with him in the first place because I didn't want to be rude, but he made my flesh crawl right from the start with his chalky white face and vacant expression. Well, I say chalky, but really his complexion had more of a moist sheen to it and his eyes seemed colourless. He was just one of those people: you know it's not fair to condemn them straight away, but I put him down as ignorant as soon as he opened his mouth. The conversation went something like this:

Him: I'm called Dean, and what's *your* name?

Me: Julia.

Him: Julie, that's a nice name.

Me: No. Julia.

Him: (Leaning forward so that his ear was right beside my mouth.) Pardon? (He stank of whisky and cigarettes.)

Me: Julia.

Him: Where do you work, Julie?

Me: Barclay's Bank.

Him: Ooh! Who's the clever one, then?

I felt an urgent need to get far away from him, so when the song was finished, I said a polite 'Thank you,' and escaped to the kitchen, where I stuffed a sausage roll into my mouth to take the bad taste away. Well, you wouldn't believe it, but when I was getting my coat on to go home, he appeared again and asked me if I'd go to the pictures with him. I mean, how dense was he? I said a quick, 'No thank you. My taxi's waiting outside,' and hurried off.

Now here was my dear friend Jane introducing the slimeball as her boyfriend.

'Hi everyone,' said Jane. 'This is Dean. Dean, this is Lisa.' Lisa gave her usual friendly grin and clasped his outstretched hand.

'This is Jill,' continued Jane. Jill shook his hand, but I saw a flicker of doubt in her eyes.

'And this is Julia,' said Jane.

'Pleased to meet you,' said Dean, squeezing my hand in both of his. Ugh! He didn't show any sign of recognising me, and I struggled not to let the revulsion that had shot through me at his touch show on my face.

Now, the thing about Jane was that she was desperate to get married and have kids. She'd been going out with a really nice guy for a year but she was too clingy, and he'd got cold feet and dumped her. She had quite a broad face with small eyes and mousy hair, and men weren't attracted to her at first sight. She'd been out with guys who'd got to know her at the hospital where she worked in admin. We were all in our mid-thirties and Jane was very aware of her biological clock ticking. It seemed that she was so broody that she was willing to take anyone, which was quite upsetting.

I'd known Jane since we started school, and it bothered me to see her with him. I felt worried for her, and not just because of his lack of intelligence.

Lisa and Jane threw themselves into entertaining him with the old stories about school and holidays, but I could tell that Jill, like me, was startled by this bottom-of-the-barrel choice of Jane's, so we chatted quietly to each other about her work at the chemist's and swapped stories about difficult customers. Then Dean's high-pitched voice called over,

'Life and souls of the party you two, aren't you?'

Jill and I forced a smile, and Jill took the plunge with,

'What do you do for a living, Dean?'

'Oooh! Miss Look-After-Your-Friend, aren't you?' he said, making quote marks in the air. 'Frightened I'm a bank robber, are you? I'm an entrepreneur, if you must know,' he said, only he pronounced it 'enter prenure'.

There was silence at that, until the ever-lovely Lisa laughed cheerily, and asked who'd like another drink.

Friday 12ᵗʰ May, 1989

I ran upstairs when I got home, with the joy of it being the weekend. I opened the door, and whack! It hit me: Old Spice. It's hard to describe it, but if you can imagine what it would be like to be whisked back in time and dumped into your long-lost childhood home, then maybe you can feel what I did. I was standing at the front door, trying to get a grip of my emotions, when old Mrs. Fairweather from upstairs spoke right behind me and made me jump.

'Are you all right, dear?'

I turned round.

'You look as if you've seen a ghost,' she said.

Smelt one more like, I thought but, 'Can you smell aftershave?' I asked, gesturing towards my hall. She stuck her head through the door.

'Oh, yes. Old Spice isn't it?' she asked. 'All the men used to wear it.'

'Does Mr. Fairweather wear it?' I asked. She laughed and said,

'Not since Neil Armstrong walked on the Moon. Someone must have been along with it on. Maybe the postman, out to impress.'

She laughed again, and made her slow way upstairs. There was no post for me.

It was stronger this time. I sniffed about like a police dog but I couldn't work it out. It just didn't make sense. The walls and doors stank of it, but the plugholes didn't. Anyway, I'd got bacon for tea, so the smell took my mind off it, and I watched *My Fair Lady* as an end-of-week treat, and went to bed early.

I had such a weird dream about Dad. I was in our old back garden playing on the swing, trying to go as high as possible, when he came out, all dressed up in his dark brown suit and thin, bottle-green tie, his curly black hair all shiny in the sun.

'Be careful,' he urged. 'You're going too high. You'll fall off and get hurt one of these days.'

I stopped working my legs, and let the swing slow down a bit, then I jumped off and sailed through the air. I landed right beside him and he looked a bit cross.

'You jumped off too soon,' he said. Then he smiled in his usual crinkly way that made me feel all warm and comfortable.

'I'm off now. Give us a hug.' He picked me up, gave me a quick cuddle, swung me round and I breathed in that familiar smell of my dear Old Spice Dad. Then I woke up.

Saturday, 13ᵗʰ May, 1989.

Well, I expect that you can imagine how I felt: disappointed, empty, a bit sorry for myself, so I got up and went straight to the shower to wash it away. I ran the water until it was really hot, the bathroom all steamy, and then dried myself with a good vigorous rub to get rid of that dream. I was quite pleased with myself, even started to feel chirpy, but then I looked up from drying my feet and had the shock of my life. On the mirror in bold block capitals I saw these letters standing out in the steam:

BE C&REFUL

I fell down as if someone had punched me, and sat there on the floor, staring. My heart was racing, and I was shivering, suddenly freezing. I pulled the towel round me, whimpering like a terrified puppy, and

I'll tell you why. See, it wasn't just the fact that someone had been in there writing a message on my mirror that would only show up when it was steamy, it was the fact that the message could only have been written by my Dad. Yes, I know. It was crazy, wasn't it? Let me explain.

One day when I was about eight years old, Dad was writing some cheques. He explained about signatures. He said you had to decide what yours would be and always write it the same way. I thought I'd have a shot at mine. After a few tries, I started doing daft ones: ones with faces in the B, ones where some of the letters had fallen over. Then Dad joined in, but he only did one silly one and it was:

R&YMOND B&RR

So I copied him and did:

JULI& B&RR

They sort of stuck. We used to leave notes for each other signed R&Y and JULI&. Mum couldn't join in because there was no 'A' in her name. She was called Iris, so it was just a joke between the two of us.

Anyway, what with the dream and the smell of Old Spice and everything, I knew it was Dad, come back to warn me about something. You may not want to believe me, but I was convinced, right through my bones, that he was trying to protect me from something, so I kept thinking what it could be. I made myself stop it in the end, before it drove me barmy, and went out to buy a new skirt to wear that evening.

Jill, Lisa and I went to our usual place, The Salsa Club. We all go to lessons once a week, and then it's like a big party on Saturday night. It's great. You dance with the men without having to worry about pairing off with anyone. You just enjoy the dancing. Well, while the band was having a break, and the three of us were discussing how worried we were about Jane, or rather, the ever-sensible Jill and I were, as Lisa said that she couldn't see anything to worry about, who should come in but Jane herself, with the ghastly Dean in tow. Talk about putting a damper on things! I said as friendly a hello as I could manage, and squashed up to make room for them round the table.

Luckily it was only a few minutes before the band came back on, and Jane got Dean up to show off her moves. The rest of us had a couple of dances, and then were happy to sit and watch for a while.

Jane and Dean came back, and then Dean made a great big show of asking Lisa to dance, all gentlemanly and slimy. Lisa giggled and went off with him. Jane watched them like a hawk. Lisa's good: got all the sexy hip movements, and makes it look so easy. Dean was useless, with no sense of rhythm at all. In the end he just stood still, and let her hold his hands and dance in front of him.

He brought her back after one dance and bowed to Jill, holding his hand out to her. She looked a bit reluctant, but took hold of it. Jane looked slightly less worried. Jill was keeping as much space between Dean and herself as possible, and her smile looked a bit false. I wondered whether I could get away with turning down his request if he asked me, but decided it would look rude.

Sure enough, back he came with Jill, and held his hand out to me. I started dancing like I'd seen Jane doing, keeping a good distance away from him, then all of a sudden he pulled me towards him and swung me round, clutching me to his chest and keeping me there. He was really strong, and though I tried to push him off, I couldn't get free. I felt the same repulsion rush through me as I had felt at the party. He danced me round on the spot for a few seconds then,

'How's it going at the bank, Julie?' he asked, exaggerating the word 'bank' as if it was Hollywood or something. He sneered at me, or maybe it was a knowing smile.

'Fine,' I said, not wanting him to think that I was bothered by his remembering me.

'Seen any good films lately?' he asked in that sarcastic tone.

'No,' I said.

'Liar,' he said, and his voice took on a cold, menacing tone.

'What about the one you saw with Jane? The very one I asked you to go to with me.'

Oh no… *Rain Man…*

'You didn't say which one you…,' I began.

'You didn't give me a chance did you, you stuck-up bitch?'

This was edging towards something nasty.

'Well, Jane's my friend,' I said.

The music stopped. He looked at me as if he was looking at a cockroach, and then leaned forward and whispered in my ear, 'Jane *was* your friend.' Then he turned and walked away, and I was left standing there registering the fact that he was wearing Old Spice.

Monday, 15ᵗʰ May, 1989.

I rang Jane from work. I was worried about what she was letting herself in for. I mean someone who is going to take offence so easily is a bit of a dodgy candidate as a boyfriend, don't you think? I was also pondering on Dad's warning and was sure that I could feel his warm presence beside me, while inside I felt as if a gentle balm was soothing that knot of anxiety that is my usual companion. My pillow had smelt of Old Spice when I woke up, and I'd seen his message again, still there on the mirror. Was it one Old Spice wearer warning me about another? I felt that I should pass on Dad's warning to Jane. I rang her office at the hospital and recognised her voice when she answered the phone herself.

'Hi Jane,' I said. 'It's Julia.'

'Hi,' she said. 'Phoning to apologise?'

'What do you mean?' I asked.

'The way you were throwing yourself at Dean,' she said. 'He told me all about it, and I could see it for myself. He told me about what you did to him at that party as well. He's mine, Julia. Just keep your hands off,' and she put the phone down.

Oh Lord, he was ignorant and vicious with it. Goodness knows what he'd told her I'd done. I was hurt by my old friend's harsh words but it seemed useless to try calling her again, so I just left it.

When I got home the smell was even stronger. I was a bit unsettled, but felt safe, being convinced by now that my guardian angel of a dad was looking after me.

'It's OK, Dad,' I said out loud. 'I know what the message meant.' I had a little laugh at myself and went to heat up the curry that I'd got for tea.

Wednesday, 17th May, 1989.

I was taking three days' leave as a birthday treat. I do it every year as there's no one else to make a fuss of me. The postman rang the bell while I was eating my breakfast. He wanted me to sign for a registered letter from Great Aunt Winnie. She was my last remaining relation, so she made a point of sending me a postal order for my birthday, even though she was in an old folks' home. She had sent me a very generous £50, so I decided to go out and spend it as part of the day's celebrations.

I was in the hall, just about to open the door, when a nauseous fear clenched my throat. Someone was putting a key into my front door lock. Panic shot through me, and my legs turned so weak and jelly-like that I thought I couldn't move. I threw my arms forward, and to my relief, my legs followed.

In that tiny flat there was only one place to hide. Behind the front door, and opposite the bathroom was a cupboard, big enough to walk into, and by the greatest of luck, fitted with handles on both sides of the door. I opened it just wide enough to get in, and as the front door opened, the cupboard door behind it shut.

My hiding place door was made from ill-fitting planks of wood, and it was easy to see through the cracks. I struggled to breathe quietly, as my heart was thumping and I was forcing myself not to whimper. I prayed that the intruder wouldn't hear me.

I shut one eye and peeped out.

A figure crept along the hall with its back to me. It was wearing a hood, and seemed to be holding a cloth or hanky in one hand and a container in the other.

It wiped the cloth over the walls and then poured more liquid on to the cloth and reached up to wipe it over the light bulb. It went into the bathroom and turned to face the mirror. It took the hood off.

Dean!

Of course.

He stood looking at himself, then lifted a finger and wrote something with it on the mirror, and continued wiping the cloth round the walls and door.

He went into the bedroom.

My heart thumped.

He came out and went into the living room.

I took a couple of deep breaths while he was in there, and tried to be silent again.

He came back into the hall, tipping and wiping again as he came towards me. I could smell it now: Old Spice of course. Inside my head I sent up a silent prayer, *please don't open the door, please don't open the door.*

He put the top on the bottle and put the cloth in his pocket. I could see his face so close to mine as he looked around the hall, and waited in dread of the moment when he'd peer through the crack in the door and see me.

Time stalled.

Dean paused.

I waited. Then he sneered, opened the front door and went out.

I shot out of that cupboard and slid the bolt on the front door into place as quietly as my trembling hand would let me. My knees gave way, and I crawled through to the living room to find the telephone directory. My hands were shaking so much that I knocked the receiver off the phone and had to lie down beside it to call the locksmith. Then I lay there and cried like I hadn't done since I was ten years old.

After the locksmith had been and I'd spent Great Aunt Winnie's cheque on a real burglar-proof lock, I felt safe and began to relax a bit. I went into the bathroom and ran the shower until the room was steamy, and there was his message:

& REFUS&L M&Y OFFEND

What?!

All this because I wouldn't go to the cinema with him? All this because I only had one dance with him? How had he managed it?

I made a coffee and sat down to think. The caffeine must have got my brain working because, after a while, memories came to me. The first one was quite recent. Jane and I had agreed to keep a key for each other in case we locked ourselves out by accident. It took a while for the next one to surface. It was from long ago. One rainy day when we couldn't go out to play, she was round at our place, as she often was, and we were doing the silly signatures. Dad came in, and we showed Jane our special messages, and she did one herself with her name, J&NE.

Once I'd got going, the next memory came quickly. We were talking about boys and how they smelt funny, but how our Dads had nice smells. I said that mine smelt of Old Spice, which I suppose she already knew, and she said that her Dad smelt of pipe smoke. She'd told Dean, but why, for goodness sake? Maybe they were bitching about me. He must have pumped her for information, invented ways in which I'd offended him. Maybe she was jealous of me, though I can't think why. Maybe he was a stalker or, heaven forbid, something worse!

I didn't go out for the rest of my time off work. I suppose you're wondering why I didn't call Jill or Lisa, but I'd always been closer to Jane, and anyway, I was used to working things out on my own. I felt a bit of a fool for having believed that Dad had come back to warn me about something, and to be honest, I was very disappointed and sad that he hadn't. Instead, that repellent creep had used my happy memories to frighten the life out of me. It was as if I'd lost Dad all over again. That's why I did all the crying, that's why I didn't want to see anyone.

Saturday 17ᵗʰ June, 1989.

The phone rang while I was still asleep.

'Julia, it's Lisa. Are you awake?'

'Well I am now.'

'You'll never guess what's happened,' she said.

'Tell me.'

'Dean's been stabbed. Are you there Julia? Julia?'

'Yes, sorry, yes, just, oh good grief, it's such a shock!'

'He's dead, Julia. Someone got into a fight with him in the pub. He said that Dean owed him money. Dean just laughed and walked away but when he got outside the guy came after him and started shouting, and said he was sick of waiting for it. Dean told him to get lost, and the guy stabbed him. Jane's hysterical. I'm round at hers now and her mum's here. Who'd have thought it, Julia? Poor Jane!'

You shouldn't be glad when someone dies but I have to admit that I was relieved. Well, wouldn't you have been? I'd been so frightened of what might happen next, like a knife between the ribs, or strangulation.

I put the local radio station on that evening, just after the news had started and heard:

'Local man, Dean Jackson, was stabbed in the Grassmarket last night, after what is reported to have been an argument in a nearby public house about debt. Police are searching for a man who disappeared from the scene shortly after the incident. The man was described as being in his late thirties, with dark curly hair. He was wearing a brown suit and a thin, bottle-green tie. The barmaid said that neither she nor any of the regulars had ever seen him before. She said she'd worked there for over twenty years and some customers had been coming to the pub long before she got the job. She said that he'd sat on his own at the bar and introduced himself to her as Ray. She added that he smelt as if he'd used half a bottle of Old Spice aftershave. Anyone having any information about this man should contact their local police station immediately.'

January 1999.

Nobody ever came forward with any more information, and the murderer has never been found. The case remains open but, almost, forgotten.

Hamlet and John

Olga Wojtas

Hamlet and John

From the children's book 'Hamlet and John'.

This is Hamlet. This is John. They are in the park.

'See how high I can go on the swing, Hamlet!' says John. 'Come and play on the swings!'

But Hamlet cannot decide whether to play on the swings or the roundabout.

'We must be home by four o'clock,' says John. 'Can you tell the time, Hamlet?'

'No,' says Hamlet, 'but I can tell a hawk from a handsaw.'

'That must be very useful,' says John.

Here comes Janet. 'Hello, John,' says Janet.

'Hello, Janet,' says John.

'Hello, Hamlet,' says Janet. 'Do you love me?'

'No,' says Hamlet. 'No, Janet, I do not love you. Go away.'

Janet goes away. She is crying. She does not see the pond.

Look out, Janet!

Run, John! Run, Hamlet!

It is too late.

'Janet is dead,' says John. 'I am very sad.'

'I am more sad than you,' says Hamlet.

'You cannot be more sad than me, Hamlet,' says John. 'I am Janet's brother.'

'I am more sad than forty thousand brothers,' says Hamlet.

'Forty thousand?' says John. 'That is a very big number. I can only count up to ten.'

THE END

ACKNOWLEDGEMENTS

We have to thank our former tutor, Colin Mortimer, for planting the seed of the idea that we should, as a group, publish our work. To be fair he actually planted many seeds over the years but most of them fell on the stony ground of our individual prevarication, insecurity, or perhaps just laziness.

In our time with him, Colin inspired, encouraged, gently cajoled, positively criticised, and generally supported us to become better writers. More than that, he gave us the opportunity to learn from, and create friendships with, individuals with different backgrounds, styles, abilities and personalities. We feel privileged not only to have had Colin as our tutor but to have gained such long-standing friends.

One of our group did manage to grow and successfully grasp the nettle of publication, but for the remainder it took the arrival of Gordon Lawrie with his skills, knowledge, and experience of publishing, to push us finally into action. With patience, determination, humour, and scrupulous attention to detail, Gordon has enabled this book to be published. We owe him a huge debt.

We also owe a debt to one of our group, Andrew Licudi, for taking us in after Colin retired, and for his exemplary hospitality. We are lucky to have a true wine expert in our midst!

We are also fortunate to benefit from the artistic skills of Gerry Webber, another member of the group. Gerry did the sketch of the typewriter on the cover and surprised at least some of us with his amazing talent.

A group of nine writers can, to some extent, do its own proofreading, allocating each writer's story to one of its other members. For all that, mistakes still slip through and we are indebted to Heather Simpson for giving us the benefit of her professional experience and skills in that area. Nevertheless, the end result, warts and all, remains the collective responsibility of Auld Reekie Scrievers.

Acknowledgements

There is a quote from Erica Jong:

"I went for years not finishing anything. Because, of course, when you finish something you can be judged."

We hope you enjoy dipping into our collection.

The Auld Reekie Scrievers

THE AULD REEKIE SCRIEVERS

Lesley Henderson was born in Edinburgh and currently lives in Edinburgh with her husband and dog. Her three grown-up children are scattered around the globe. She was a social worker and social work manager in London, the Borders, the Lothians and Edinburgh until she retired. She has been writing short stories for the last seven years and this is her first published work.

Norma Hurley came late to writing fiction. Although, since she spent much of her career writing publications for UK and European governments, some might say she was always imaginative. She studied Italian at university in Edinburgh and now spends as much time as she can between there and her home in Tuscany. Her stories were selected from those written during ten plus years in the company of the Auld Reekie Scrievers.

Andrew Licudi was born and raised in Gibraltar and now lives in Edinburgh. He has lived in Spain and spent two years in Algeria on an old sailboat. An engineer by profession, Andrew is also a vinophile and has written over sixty wine articles for various magazines, including Jancis Robinson, where he was twice shortlisted in Robinson's International Wine Writing Competition. Currently, Andrew writes short stories inspired by the places he has lived and worked.

Liz Logie MacIver, originally from Dundee, has been writing short stories for 15 years. Her love of the written word began early in life, blossoming during her studies in Aberdeen and Edinburgh. Her career involved sales marketing and business, culminating in academic work focusing on the psychology of why we buy products and services. She lives in the south side of Edinburgh. She is married, has two children and three grandchildren.

American-born but raised in Fife, **Chester Simpson** came to Edinburgh as a student and never left. Married with two grown-up daughters, he spent most of his working life in IT in financial services. Life-long interests include football, American history and long-distance walking. It was while maintaining a journal on the Appalachian Trail, and with no literary qualifications whatsoever, that he thought he might one day try writing short story fiction. Much of this has been in the company of the Auld Reekie Scrievers.

Sherri Underwood writes thought-provoking stories about the dark, sometimes uncomfortable sides of family life. She lives in St Andrews with her husband and her poodle, Isla. Besides creative writing, Sherri spends her time on long dog walks and taming her wild Scottish garden. She has two grown daughters who live in England and provide encouragement and occasionally also material for her stories.

Judith Wall is to be found enjoying her retirement in theatres, cinemas, bookshops and with her writing group. She can be spotted walking in the countryside, visiting castles or stately homes or just admiring the scenery. She lived and taught in various parts of England and Scotland. Friends say she is an honorary Scot but having lived in Edinburgh for forty years, she now considers herself a true 'Auld Reekie Scriever'.

Gerry Webber lives in Edinburgh and writes for fun. He has published a number of short stories, several of which have appeared in prize anthologies. God loves a trier. One day he might win. Much of his work is darkly humorous. Most of his work is thankfully short.

Olga Wojtas, born and brought up in Edinburgh, is one of the few people who can both spell and pronounce her Polish surname. A journalist for most of her life, she is a news junkie but finds it quite depressing and turns to fiction as escapism. She writes the *Miss Blaine's Prefect* comic crime novels about a 50-something time-travelling Morningside librarian, and also the *Bunburry* cosy crime e-novellas under the name Helena Marchmont.

Editor

Gordon Lawrie has lived in Edinburgh all of his life. He worked for 36 years as a secondary school teacher before redundancy presented the opportunity to try his hand at writing fiction. The author of five novels and a collection of his own short stories, he's also the editor of the worldwide online weekly publication Friday Flash Fiction. His wife has spent many, many hours gazing at the inverted lid of a laptop.

Dean Park Press

An imprint of the innovative Comely Bank Publishing self-publishing collective, Dean Park Press is an Edinburgh-based micro-publisher that specialises in the fiction output of local writers.